JAPJEE

SIKH MORNING PRAYER

ੴ

JAPJEE

SIKH MORNING PRAYER

Translated by:

Khushwant Singh

Picus
BOOKS

First Published in India by:
Picus Books
C-30, West End
New Delhi-110 021

First Reprint	2000
Second Reprint	2001
Third Reprint	2002
Fourth Reprint	2004

Designed by Ilaksha – Picus Art Studio

Printed and bound at
Thomson Press (India) Ltd.

Exclusive Distributors:
THE VARIETY BOOK DEPOT
A.V.G. Bhawan, M-3, Connaught Circus
New Delhi-110 001
Fax: 23415335

CONTENTS

PREFACE

There are over fifteen million Sikhs in the world. Prior to the partition of India in 1947 most of them lived in the Punjab. Since then almost two million have had to leave their homes and possessions in the area which went to Pakistan. The vast majority of them are now in Eastern Punjab, which came to the share of India.

The Sikhs now face the great danger of a challenge to their very existence as a separate community. The pattern of nation-building in a country like India has inevitably to be a secular one. Privileges based on racial or religious considerations find no place in it. During British rule the Sikhs enjoyed a number of such privileges. The system of separate electorates provided them with political representation in excess of their numerical strength. In the Services, particularly the army, the authorities themselves insisted on the observance of the forms and symbols of Sikhism for persons holding posts reserved for Sikhs. In the universities, their language and script enjoyed the same status as that of the other communities. Thus, political, economic and cultural safeguards provided the Sikhs with a sort of hot-house existence for over a century. Now the economic motives behind the observances of such Sikh symbols as unshorn hair and beard have gone. Separate electorates have been abolished. Hindi has been declared to be the official language for all Indians. The Sikhs fight a losing battle and a generation or two may have lost their distinctive identity as a separate community and become like the Jains, Brahmo Samajists, Arya Samajists or Sanatists, a sub-section of the Hindu social system. Circumstances may, however, once again arouse the dynamic interest in the teachings of the Gurus, and the Sikh faith spread itself "as oil on the waters" of India. Both these possibilities make the study of the Sikhs and their religion important. My purpose is only to give a brief account of the Sikh Gurus and their teachings, particularly with reference to their morning prayer. The earlier works by Malcolm, Murray and Wilson were written without any first-hand knowledge of the Sikh religion. The first serious attempt to write about Sikh religion was undertaken by the India Office as early as 1869. Dr. Ernest Trumpp, a German missionary and philologist, was commissioned to produce a translation of the Sikh holy scripture, the *Granth Sahib*. He was not very successful in his work. After two years of research he came to the conclusion that "the language of the *Granth* had become already obsolete to a great extent." He got very little assistance from Sikh scholars—indeed, he was sure that none existed. "The Sikhs," he wrote, "in consequence of their former warlike manner of life and troublous times, had lost all their learning." When Dr. Trumpp's translation finally appeared, in 1877, it proved offensive to Sikh susceptibilities. In order to repair the damage caused to "the loyal Sikhs" M.A. Macauliffe was commissioned to undertake the work. Macauliffe described Trumpp's work as "highly inaccurate and unidiomatic... Whenever he saw an opportunity of defaming the Gurus, the sacred book and the religion of the Sikhs, he eagerly availed himself of it." Macauliffe confessed that the object of his work was "to make reparations to the Sikhs... without criticism or expression of opinion of his own."

It is obvious that neither Trumpp nor Macauliffe possessed the degree of objectivity necessary for undertaking. It must, however, be added in fairness to Macauliffe that his is the only literal translation of the *Granth Sahib* in existence and as such is invaluable as a book of reference. There are many small books on the Sikhs and their religion written both by Englishmen and Indians. Apart from Cunningham's *History of the Sikhs*, most of the English works have been in the nature of guide books for the use of their countrymen attached as officers to Sikh regiments. The writings of Indians, specially the Sikhs, have been primarily addressed to their own people—and even when written in English assume knowledge of Indian mythology and the Hindu-Muslim conflict which forms the background to the Sikh faith. This makes them unintelligible to the average English reader. I am convinced that, however sympathetic one may be to another's view of life (as indeed was Macauliffe towards the Sikhs), there remains a feeling of fatuity about any faith except one's own. I have therefore ventured to present this brief account of the Sikh religion and the morning prayer in the hope that they may be seen from the point of view of a Sikh who believes both in the Sikh faith and in objectivity.

KHUSHWANT SINGH

THE SIKH FAITH AND PRACTICE

In the life of every nation there comes a time when accepted values begin to be questioned. This is usually occasioned by a challenge from another set of values at variance with those formerly accepted. The conflict may result in compromise and the emergence of a new code of living incorporating principles common to both systems. Sometimes the new code finds adherents who break away from their original loyalties to form a new community bound by allegiance to a new way of life. The Sikhs are an example of the emergence of a community with a communal consciousness fashioned out of new social norms.

For several centuries Indians accepted Hinduism as something ordained and immutable. From 780 A.D. began Muslim invasions from the north. The invaders' religion and way of life were the antithesis of whatever Hinduism stood for. Their religion was a simple set of do's and don'ts, most of them with direct bearing on matters of everyday life. A large part of the *Koran* consisted of rules on what a man may or may not eat and drink, how many wives he may marry, how to treat them and divorce them. The faith itself was brief and simple—that there was one God and Mohammed was his Prophet. The *Koran* was the word of God and what it said was law unto mankind. The *Koran* insisted on the unity of God in opposition to Hindu pantheism; it deified the iconoclast in a country of idol-worshippers; it stood for the equality of men in a country ridden with caste distinctions; it sanctioned pleasures of the flesh and palate in a country which preached the ascetic ideal.

For seven centuries Islam and Hinduism battled for supremacy. There were periods when Islam, with characteristic impatience, argued sword in hand. Hinduism with characteristic resilience withstood persecution and took the edge off the Islamic sword. By the fifteenth century in India had many million Muslims—but by then Muslims were observing caste distinctions, visiting Hindu temples, and generally accepting Hindu customs and conventions. Above all, they accepted the principles of religious tolerance. On the other side, the Hindus themselves recognised the superiority of the concept of the indivisibility of the Godhead, of the evils of caste and other unwholesome social customs. The stage was set for the emergence of a school of thought propagating a fusion of faiths based on principles common to Islam and Hinduism. This was the school of Bhagta Philosophy.

Like the religious reformation in Europe, the Bhagta movement in India was basically a protest against religious dogma, ritual and intolerance. The propounders of *Bhakta* philosophy—Ramananda, Gorakhnath, Chaitanya, Kabir, Tulsi Das, Vallabh and Namdev—taught that the form and place of worship were of little consequence; that basically Hinduism and Islam had the same values, only the nomenclature was different. They evolved a form of religious poetry with a vocabulary which borrowed liberally from the sacred texts of both Hindus and Muslims. It had a spontaneity which appealed to the masses. All that the movement lacked was personal leadership and guidance. This was provided by Guru Nanak (1469–1539), the founder of the Sikh faith.

Guru Nanak, like the other *Bhakta* philosophers, was more concerned with spreading religious tolerance than with founding a new community. His teachings, however, fired the imagination of the Punjab peasantry and even during his lifetime a large number of followers gathered round him.

At first they were merely known as his disciples (in Sanskrit "*Shishya*"). Some time later these disciples became a homogeneous group whose faith was exclusively the teachings of Nanak. The *Shishya* became the "Sikh" (corruption of the Sanskrit word).

Guru Nanak was content to be a teacher. He laid no claims to divinity or to kinship with God. He did not invest his writings with the garb of prophecy nor his word with the sanctity of a "message." His teaching was a crusade against cant and humbug in religion and his life was patterned by what he said was eminently well said, as his hymns are the finest in the Punjabi language. What he did was eminently well done, because his life was an example of his faith.

He ignored religious and caste distinctions and took as his associates a Muslim musician and a low caste Hindu. He ridiculed such Hindu religious practices as gave importance to bathing in "sacred" rivers, wearing "sacred" threads, and making offerings to dead ancestors. He personally went to these places of pilgrimage and demonstrated to worshippers their utter absurdity. Likewise he went on pilgrimage to Muslim shrines and reprimanded priests who made a trade of religion and transgressed the injunctions of the *Koran*. His success in efforts to bring Hindus and Muslims together was a personal one. He was acclaimed by both communities, and on his death they clamoured for his body—the Muslims wanted to bury him, the Hindus to cremate him. Even today he is regarded in the Punjab as a symbol of harmony between Hindus and Muslims. A popular couplet describes him:

Guru Nanak the King of Fakirs,
To the Hindu a Guru, to the Muslims a Pir

In fifty years of travel and teaching Guru Nanak had attracted a following which could at best be described as a group dissenting from both Hinduism and Islam. It was left to his successors to mould this group into a community with its own language and literature, religious beliefs and institutions, traditions and conventions.

Guru Nanak was followed by nine other Gurus. Succession was determined on the basis of finding a teacher most fitted to safeguard and develop the spiritual legacy left by Nanak. Hence for two centuries there was remarkable continuity in the functions of leadership. These years saw the consummation of the religious aspect of Sikhism. They also saw nascent Hindu nationalism grow to political power and pave the way to the setting up of a Sikh State. Of the ten Gurus, the second, fourth, sixth and tenth were chiefly responsible for measures which fostered communal consciousness and welded the Sikhs into an independent community.

On the Hindu New Year's day in 1699, the tenth, Guru Gobind Singh, assembled his followers and initiated five, known as the *Punj Piyaras*, into a new fraternity which he named the *Khalsa* or "the pure." Of these five, one was a Brahmin, one a *Kshatrya*, and three belonged to the lower castes. They were made to drink out of the same bowl and given new names with the suffix "Singh" (lion) attached to them. They swore to observe the "Five K's"—namely, to wear their hair and beard unshorn (*kesh*); to carry a comb in the hair (*kungha*); to wear a pair of shorts (*kuchha*); to wear a steel bangle on the right wrist (*kara*); and to carry a sword (*kirpan*). The Khalsa were also enjoined to observe four rules of conduct (*rahat*): not to cut the hair; abstain from smoking tobacco and consuming alcoholic drinks; not to eat kosher meat; and refrain from carnal intercourse with Muslims. Ever since that day every Sikh youth when he comes of age is initiated into the Khalsa by the baptism (*pahul*) of the sword and the Suffix "Singh" is attached to his name. Thereafter he has no caste save one, the fraternity of the Khalsa. The reason which prompted Guru Gobind Singh to introduce forms and symbols has never been adequately explained. Neither he nor any of his contemporaries refer to the subject in their writings. Some of them are, however, intelligible in their historical background.

Guru Gobind Singh completed the religious facet of Sikhism. He turned an innocuous band of pacifists into armed crusaders. Those who did not accept his innovations of forms and symbols remained just Sikhs, usually described as *Sahaj Dharis* or "the easy-going"; those who did became the *Khalsa*. Guru Gobind Singh lost all his four sons in the struggle against the Muslim rulers and declared the succession of Gurus at an end. The Sikhs were to look to the *Adi Granth* for spiritual guidance, which was henceforth to be the symbolic representation of the ten Gurus. Ceremonies and customs distinct from those of the Hindus were made current. Thus the Sikhs became a new community with an independent entity.

THE SIKH RELIGION

By legislative enactment a Sikh has been defined as "one who believes in the ten Gurus and the *Granth Sahib*." This definition is not exhaustive. There are people who call themselves Sikhs who do not believe in all the ten Gurus. There are others who believe that the line of Gurus continued after the tenth and follow the precepts of a living Guru. Similarly, some Sikhs challenge the authenticity of certain passages of the *Granth Sahib*, while others insist on including extraneous writing in it. Besides these, there are numerous sub-sects distinguished by allegiance to one or other Guru or claiming that the real Guru had been overlooked in deciding the succession. Despite these discrepant factors, it can be safely asserted that the belief in the ten Gurus and the authorised version of the *Granth Sahib* is the common basic factor of the Sikh faith, and it covers the vast majority of Sikhs. The only practical sectional division of the Sikh community is into the orthodox Khalsa and the clean-shaven *Sahaj Dhari*.

CONCEPTION OF GOD

The Sikh religion, as enunciated in the scriptures, is a wholesome mixture of Islamic sufi doctrines and Hindu mystic philosophy. It inculcates belief in the unity of God and equates God with truth. The preamble to the morning prayer Japjee, which is recited as an introduction to all religious ceremonies and is known as the *Mool Mantra*, the basic belief, states:

There is one God.
He is the supreme truth.
He, the creator,
Is without fear and without hate.
He, the omnipresent,
Pervades the universe.
He is not born,
Nor does He die to be reborn again.

Before Time itself
There was truth.
When Time began to run its course He was the truth.
Even now, He is the truth.

Evermore shall truth persist.

(NANAK)

The tenth Guru, Gobind Singh, ventured farther into philosophic speculation in describing God as *akalpurukh* (timeless):

Time is the only God,
The Primal and the final,
The creator and the destroyer.
How can words describe him?

God has no form or substance. He is *nirunkar* (formless). Although He is beyond human comprehension, by righteous living one can invoke His grace.

In the first verse of the morning prayer Guru Nanak said:

Not by thought alone
Can he be known,
Tho' one think a hundred thousand times
Not in solemn silence,
Nor in deep meditation.
Though fasting yields an abundance of virtue,
No! by none of these
Nor by a hundred thousand other devises
Can God be reached.
How then shall truth be known?
How the veil of false illusion torn?
O Nanak, thus runneth the writ divine.
The righteous path let it be thine.

The Sikh religion expressly forbids the worship of idols and emblems as Gods in no uncertain terms:

They that worship strange Gods
Cursed shall be their lives, cursed their habitations,

Poison shall be their food—each morsel,
Poisoned too shall be their garments.
In life for them is misery, In life hereafter, hell.

(AMAR DAS—third Guru)

Some worship stones and on their heads they bear them,
Some the phallus—strung in necklaces wear its emblem.
Some behold their God in the South,
some to the West bow their head,
Some worship images, others busy praying to the dead.
The world is thus bound in false ritual
And God's secret is still unread.

(GURU GOBIND)

Guru Nanak, while attending the evening service at a Hindu temple where a salver full of small oil lamps and incense was being waved in front of the idol before it was laid to rest for the night, composed this verse:

The firmament is thy salver
The Sun and Moon thy lamps,
The galaxy of stars
Are as pearls scattered.
The woods of sandal are thy incense
The forests thy flowers
But what worship is this,
O Destroyer of Fear?

THE GURU OR THE TEACHER

God being an abstraction, godliness is conceived more as an attribute than a concrete something which can be acquired by a person or a thing. The way of acquiring godliness or salvation is to obey the will of God. The means of ascertaining God's will are, as in other theological systems, unspecified and subject to human speculation. They are largely rules of moral conduct which are the basis of human society. Sikh religion advocates association with men of religion for guidance. Hence the importance of the Guru or the teacher and the institution of discipleship.

Sikhs do not worship human beings as reincarnations of God. The Gurus themselves repeated that they were like other human beings and were on no account to be worshipped. Guru Nanak constantly referred to himself as the slave and servant of God. Guru Gobind Singh, who was the author of most of the Sikh practice and ritual, was conscious of the danger of having divinity imposed on him by his followers. He explained his mission in life:

For though my thoughts were lost in prayer
At the feet of Almighty God,
I was ordained to establish a sect and lay down its rules.
But whosoever regards me as Lord
Shall be damned and destroyed.
I am—and of this let there be no doubt—
I am but the slave of God, as other men are,
A beholder of the wonders of creation.

In another passage he refuted claims to divinity and reincarnation made by others—

God has no friends nor enemies.
He heeds no hallelujahs nor cares about cures.
Being the first and timeless
How could he manifest himself through those
Who are born and die?

Godliness being the aim of human endeavour, the lives and teachings of the Gurus are looked upon as aids towards its attainment.

PACIFISM AND USE OF FORCE

Sikh pacifism in religion and the Sikh militarism present a contradiction which can only be explained by a reference to history. A strictly pacifist faith is difficult to reconcile with a spartan military tradition, except through the formula that when the faith itself is threatened with extinction, force may be used to preserve it. This indeed was Guru Gobind Singh's explanation of the steps he took. In a Persian couplet he said:

Chu kar uz hama har heel te dar guzusht
Halal ust burdan ba shamsheer dust.
(When all other means have failed
It is righteous to draw the sword.)

It is possible that if the state of affairs in the Punjab had returned to a peaceful normality the Sikh sword might have been sheathed and the gospel of Nanak, which preached peace and humanity, have become symbolic of the Sikh faith. As it was, the period following Guru Gobind Singh was about the most turbulent known to Indian history. The decaying Moghul empire took to making scapegoats of minorities to explain away its failures. There were pogroms of unprecedented savagery in which the small band of Sikhs was almost exterminated. Coincident with persecution within the country came new Muslim invasions from the north, which destroyed any people or institution they deemed un-Islamic. In such circumstances martial traditions were forged which became an integral part of Sikh life and gave the Sikhs the reputation of being a fighting people.

LIFE OF GURU NANAK

'On the night of the full moon in the month of *Vaisakh* in *Samvat* 1526,' says the more authentic version – Mehervan's *Janam Sakhi* – on the life of Guru Nanak, 'Tripta, the wife of Mehta Kalian Das Bedi of Talwandi Rae Bhoe, was in labour. Three-quarters of the night had passed. The morning star shone bright in the eastern sky; it was the hour of early dawn when she was delivered of her second child, a son.'

Nanak's birth was thus on 15 April 1469. However, in order to continue an old tradition, the event is celebrated on the full moon night in the month of November. As to the place of his birth, it is thought that the name Nanak was given to the child because he was born in the house of his maternal grandparents or *nankey* which was either in Kahna Kacha or Chalewal, two villages in the district of Lahore.

It was, however, clear that the time of decision was at hand.

Nanak's days were spent in noting down receipts and expenses. At the end of the day he added up the totals to make sure they tallied with the accounts. He often had to work late into the night adding up his figures under the light of the lamp. One night he got angry with himself and threw away his pen and account books. He asked himself, 'Why have I got involved in these affairs and forgotten my Maker? Am I destined to spend my days and nights writing accounts? It is a vast net in which I find myself caught; if I let the days go by the noose will close tighter around me. If I have to burn the midnight oil, it should be for something worthwhile.'

Nanak pondered over these things late into the night and, instead of returning home, went to the stream to bathe. He prayed, 'Lord send me a guru, a guide who will show me the path that leads to Thy mansion.'

That very night God revealed Himself to Nanak. Nanak prayed fervently and begged the Lord to forgive him and remove him from the world which had so ensnared him. The Lord asked Nanak, 'Why are you so agitated? You have done no wrong.'

'I have let my mind turn from Thee,' replied Nanak, 'to the petty trifles of the world.'

'Your errors have I forgiven. The *maya* that you complain of is also a part of Me. What you see is but its shadow.'

'Lord, destroy in me the longing for worldly gain.'

'Nanak you shall no more crave for worldly gain. I am pleased with you. On you be My blessing.' [Mehervan: *Janam Sakhi*].

The mystic experience that finally made Nanak take up his mission is put at different times and is variously described. The incident took place in August 1507 on the third night before the full moon.

The moon had set, [says the *Janam Sakhi*] but it was dark and stars still twinkled in the sky when Nanak, followed by his servant, went to the river. Nanak took off his *kurta* and *dhoti* and stepped into the stream.

He closed his nostrils and ducked into the water. He did not come up. The servant waited a while and then, panicking, ran up and down the river bank crying for Nanak. A strange voice rose from the waters saying, 'Do not lose patience.'

Mardana, however, ran back to Sultanpur and sobbed out his story. A great commotion took place in the town because Nanak was loved by all–Hindus, Muslims, the rich and the poor. When Daulat Khan Lodhi heard of the mishap he was most distressed. 'Friends,' he said, 'Nanak was a man of God. Let us dredge the river and rescue his corpse.'

While the people of Sultanpur were dredging the river, Nanak was conducted into the presence of God.

The Almighty gave him a bowl of milk. 'Nanak, drink this bowl,' He commanded. 'It is not milk as it may seem; this is nectar (*amrit*). It will give thee power of prayer, love of worship, truth and contentment.'

Nanak drank the nectar and was overcome. He made another obeisance. The Almighty then blessed him. 'I release thee from the cycle of birth, death and rebirth; he that sets his eyes on you with faith will be saved; he that hears your words with conviction will be helped by Me; he that you forgive will be forgiven by Me. I grant thee salvation. Nanak go back to the evil world and teach men and women to pray (*nam*), to give in charity (*dan*) and to live cleanly (*isnan*). Do good to the world and redeem it in the age of sin (*Kaliyuga*).' [Mehervan: *Janam Sakhi*].

At dawn, three days later, on the full moon in August Nanak re-emerged. Nanak was thirty-six years old and now a changed and determined man. While the people clamoured around him acclaiming him a new messiah, he paid no heed. 'What have I to do with men like these!' he said to himself. He gave away all he had to the poor. He even cast off his clothes keeping for himself only a loin-cloth. He left his home and joined a band of hermits.

Soon people began expressing themselves loudly. 'Nanak was a sensible man,' some said, 'but now he has lost his head.' 'He is stricken with the fear of the Lord,' said others, 'and is no longer himself.' 'Something in the river has bitten him,' the rest were convinced, and took to calling him 'mad, bewitched.'

'It is the Lord who has possessed me and made me mad,' explained Nanak. 'If I find merit in the eyes of my Lord, then will I have justified my waywardness.'

'Nanak, you are a different person today from what you were,' the people exclaimed. 'Tell us the path you intend to take. We only know of two ways; one of the Hindus and the other of the Mussalmans.'

'There is no Hindu, there is no Mussalman,' replied Nanak.

'You talk in cryptic language,' they said. 'In this world we understand the two ways–of Hinduism and of Islam.'

'There are no Mussalmans, there are no Hindus,' repeated Nanak. [Mehervan: *Janam Sakhi*].

Nanak spent another two years in and around Sultanpur before he forsook the habitation of men and took to the forests and solitude. The faithful Mardana was his sole companion. He took on a strange dress: a cloth cap (*seli topee*), a long cloak worn by Muslim mendicants, a beggar's bowl, staff and prayer mat. When asked why he wore this outlandish garb, Nanak replied, 'I am dressed like a clown for the amusement of my Master. If my apparel pleases Him, I will be happy.'

Nanak's first journey took him eastwards to Hindu centres of pilgrimage. His biographies have fabricated many incidents based on Nanak's hymns–many of which depict the Guru's love for nature.

One day, says Mehervan's *Janam Sakhi*, Nanak and Mardana, while travelling espied a flock of swans flying overhead. Nanak was bewitched and began to run after them with his eyes fixed on the birds. Mardana followed him. The flock descended in a field and let Nanak approach them without showing any sign of fear–for Nanak was a man of God, who harmed no one. Nanak admired the birds; their long slender necks, their luminous dark eyes and their silver-white plumage. He wondered whether these birds–who spanned the heavens–had ever cast their eyes on their Maker. Why, he asked himself, should such beautiful birds wander restlessly across the continents–from Khorasan in Central Asia to Hindustan and back again to Khorasan? He blessed the swans and bade them godspeed on their journey.

Another hymn illustrates the political and social conditions of the time through picturing an incident that occurred in the suburbs of the capital city, Delhi. The city was at the time ruled by a bloodthirsty Pathan king (Ibrahim Lodhi). Nanak's fame had preceded him and large crowds of citizens, sightseers and seekers after truth, Muslims as well as Hindus, came to see him. Near Nanak's camp was a place where beggars and mendicants were fed free of charge by the wicked king. The people told Nanak of their king's evil ways and how he expiated his sins by feeding beggars.

Nanak spoke to them, 'Listen ye children of God! This charity of the king is of no consequence; it is the act of a blind man stumbling in the dark. He is worse than a blind man because even if his eyes lose their light, a blind man can hear and speak and comprehend, but one who has lost his mind has lost all. What avail is the giving of alms to one who sins by day and gives in charity at night? A stone dam can hold the flood but if the dam bursts you cannot repair the breach by plastering mud. Evil is like the flood, the stone dam like faith. If faith weakens, the dam will give way and the flood will sweep all before it. Its force is then so great that no boat nor boatman dare embark on it to save its victims. Then nothing abides save the Name of the Lord.' [Mehervan: *Janam Sakhi*]

We do not know how long Nanaḳ stayed in Delhi. He proceeded to Hardwar on the Ganges. It was apparently at a time of some religious festival when large crowds had turned up to bathe in the 'holy' river. Mardana was very impressed with the sight and said to Nanak: 'What a lot of good people there are in the world! They must be genuinely desirous of improving themselves that brings them on a pilgrimage.'

Nanak was not so impressed by the sight of the people "washing away their sins" by the ritual of bathing. 'Only a bullion dealer can tell the difference between the genuine and the counterfeit,' he replied, 'and at this place there is no bullion dealer.'

Nanak and Mardana stayed at Hardwar for some time in order to be present at the *Baisakhi* (March-April) fair. It was on this occasion that an incident, that made Nanak famous, took place.

There was a large crowd bathing in the river. Nanak saw them face eastwards and throw palmfuls of water to the sun. Nanak entered the stream and started throwing water westwards.

'In the name of Rama!' exclaimed the shocked pilgrims, 'who is this man who throws water to the west? He is either mad or a Mussalman.' They approached Nanak and asked him why he offered water in the wrong direction. Nanak asked them why they threw it eastwards to the sun.

'We offer it to our dead ancestors,' they replied.

'Where are your dead ancestors?'

'With the gods in heaven.'

'How far is the abode of the Gods?'

'49 crore *kos* from here.'

'Does the water get that far?'

'Without doubt! But why do you throw it westwards?'

Nanak replied, 'My home and lands are near Lahore. It has rained everywhere except on my land. I am therefore watering my fields.'

'Man of God, how can you water your fields near Lahore from this place?'

'If you can send it 49 crore *kos* to the abode of the gods, why can't I send it to Lahore which is only a couple of hundred *kos* away!'

The people were abashed at this reply. 'He is not mad,' they said, 'he is surely a great seer.' [Mehervan: *Janam Sakhi*].

A large number of Hindu pilgrims who had foregathered at Hardwar became disciples of the guru. He stayed on there after the *Baisakhi* festival preaching to the people:

'The most precious gift of God is human birth because it is by reason and responsible action as human beings that we can get out of the vicious circle of life, death and rebirth and attain salvation. One must abolish duality in order to be a complete devotee.'

'And how does one overcome duality?' they asked.

'By faith in the One; by hearing and speaking of the One; by never abandoning belief in Him. By austerity, truth, restraint in his heart.' [Mehervan: *Janam Sakhi*].

From Hardwar, Nanak and Mardana proceeded to Prayag (modern Allahabad) where the rivers Jamuna and the Saraswati join the Ganges. From Prayag, the guru went to Banaras, the centre of Hindu learning and orthodoxy. The *Adi Granth* describes the many encounters Guru Nanak had with pandits who chided him for his unorthodoxy and probed his knowledge of the sacred texts.

'It matters not how many cartloads of learning you have nor what learned company you keep; it matters not how many boat-loads of books you carry nor the tree or knowledge; it matters not how many years or months you spend in study nor with what passion and single-mindedness you pursue knowledge. Only one thing really matters, the rest is but a whirlwind of the ego.'

'And what is the one thing that matters?' they asked.

Nanak replied–'There are a hundred falsehoods, but this one sovereign truth–that unless truth enters the soul all service and study is false.'

Nanak was equally forthright about the pandits' fetish of their cooking vessels and kitchens. He decided to draw their attention to this in his usual manner of highlighting the incongruous aspects.

Nanak went with them and saw with what care they bathed, scrubbed their utensils, swept the ground near the hearth, washed the vegetables and cooked the food. When one plate was laid before Nanak, he refused to eat from it. 'I am not satisfied with the purity of the food you offer me. It is prepared by one who is full of sin and sins cannot be cleansed by washing the body.'

The pandits did not fully comprehend the import of Nanak's words and prepared the meal afresh. This time they dug up the earth and re-plastered it; they even washed the logs of wood before kindling them. Again Nanak refused to partake of the meal and continued his sermon. 'You err in believing that purity can be gained by scrubbing and washing. That does not apply even to inanimate things like wood, dung-fuel or water, much less to a human being. Man is unclean when his heart is tainted with greed, his tongue coated with falsehood, his eyes envious of the beauty of another's wife or his wealth, his ears dirty with slander. All these can only be cleansed by knowledge. Basically all men are good but often they pursue a predetermined path to hell.'

Nanak was questioned on his attitude towards the

sacred texts of the Hindus: 'The *Vedas* say one thing and you another. People who read the *Vedas* do not follow their teachings and now you confuse them more than ever. Why don't you either combine your teaching with that the *Vedas* or separate them more distinctly?'

Nanak replied, 'The *Vedas* tell you of the difference between good and evil. Sin is the seed of hell; chastity the seed of paradise. Knowledge and the teaching of the *Vedas* complement each other; they are to one another as merchandise to the merchant.'

It would appear that by this time Nanak had decided that his faith was to be an eclectic one for he sang hymns of Namdev, Kabir, Ravi Dass, Sain and Beni.

His new disciples tried to persuade Nanak to settle down in Banaras. Nanak refused to do so. 'I pursue the one and only path of devotion to God,' he replied, 'your learning and religion do not appeal to me and I have no interest in trade other than the name of God for God Himself has extinguished the desire for acquisition in me.'

Piecing together evidence from other sources we find that the first journey apparently took the guru as far east as Bengal and Assam. On his way back to the Punjab, he spent some days at Jagannath Puri. He travelled round the Punjab and visited the Sufi headquarters at Pak Pattan before he set out on his second long voyage, this time southwards. He is said to have travelled through Tamil Nadu, Kerala, Konkan and Rajasthan–though there is little evidence to show that he did so.

Nanak sojourned in the Himalayas for some time before he set out on his last and longest journey. This was westwards to the Muslims' holy cities Mecca and Medina as far as Baghdad. It was on this journey that another incident took place. He was staying in a mosque and fell asleep with his feet towards the Ka'ba–an act considered of grave disrespect to the house of God. When the mullah came to say his prayers, he shook Nanak rudely and said: 'O servant of God, thou hast thy feet towards Ka'ba, the house of God; why hast thou done such a thing?'

Nanak replied: Then turn my feet towards some direction where there is no God nor the Ka'ba.'

By the time Nanak returned home, the Mughal Babar had invaded the Punjab. The Guru was at Saidpur when the town was sacked by invaders. Nanak makes many references to the havoc caused by this invasion.

Nanak was by this time too old to undertake any more strenuous journeys. He settled in the village Kartarpur where he spent the last years of his life preaching to the people. His disciples came to be known as Sikhs (from the Sanskrit *shishya* or Pali *sikkha*). He built a *dharamshala* (abode of faith) whose inmates followed a strict code of discipline: rising well before dawn, bathing and then foregathering in the *dharamshala* for prayer and hymn-singing. They went about their daily chores and met again for the evening service. At the *dharamshala* was the *guru-ka-langar* (the guru's kitchen) where all who came were obliged to break bread without distinction of caste or religion.

Among Nanak's disciples was a man called Lehna whom Nanak chose in preference to his sons as his successor. Said Nanak to Lehna: 'Thou art Angad, a part of my body,' and asked another disciple to daub Angad's forehead with saffron and proclaim him the second guru.

Nanak died in the early hours of the morning of 22 September 1539. He was a poet and lover of nature to the last. As he lay on his deathbed he recalled the scenes of his childhood. 'The *tamarisk* must be in flower now; the *pampas* grass must be waving its woolly head in the breeze; the *cicadas* must be calling in the lonely glades,' he said before he closed his eyes in eternal sleep.

Meheravan's *Janam Sakhi* records the manner his body was laid to rest. Said the Mussalmans: 'we will bury him'; the Hindus: 'we will cremate him'; Nanak said: 'you place flowers on either side, Hindus on my right, Muslims on my left. Those whose flowers remain fresh tomorrow will have their way.' He asked them to pray. When the prayer was over, Nanak pulled the sheet over him and went to eternal sleep. Next morning when they raised the sheet they found nothing. The flowers of both communities were fresh. The Hindus took theirs; the Muslims took those that they had placed.

It is little wonder that Nanak came to be revered as the king or shah of the holy men, the guru of the Hindus and the peer of the Mussalmans:

JAPJEE

ਜਪੁਜੀ जपुजी

ੴ

ਸਤਿ ਨਾਮੁ

ਕਰਤਾ ਪੁਰਖੁ

ਨਿਰਭਉ

ਨਿਰਵੈਰੁ

ਅਕਾਲ ਮੂਰਤਿ

ਅਜੂਨੀ ਸੈਭੰ

ਗੁਰ ਪ੍ਰਸਾਦਿ ॥

॥ ਜਪੁ ॥

ਆਦਿ ਸਚੁ ਜੁਗਾਦਿ ਸਚੁ ॥

ਹੈ ਭੀ ਸਚੁ ਨਾਨਕ ਹੋਸੀ ਭੀ ਸਚੁ ॥੧॥

ੴ

सति नामु

करता पुरखु

निरभउ

निरवैरु

अकाल मूरति

अजूनी सैभं

गुर प्रसादि ॥

॥ जपु ॥

आदि सचु जुगादि सचु ॥

है भी सचु नानक होसी भी सचु ॥१॥

ੴ

There is One God.
He is the supreme truth.
He, The Creator.
Is without fear and without hate.
He, The Omnipresent,
Pervades the universe.
He is not born,
Nor does he die to be born again.

By his grace
shalt thou worship him.
Before time itself
There was truth.
When time began to run its course
he was the truth.
Even now, He is the truth
And
Evermore shall truth prevail.

ਸੋਚੈ ਸੋਚਿ ਨ ਹੋਵਈ ਜੇ ਸੋਚੀ ਲਖ ਵਾਰ ॥
ਚੁਪੈ ਚੁਪ ਨ ਹੋਵਈ ਜੇ ਲਾਇ ਰਹਾ ਲਿਵ ਤਾਰ ॥
ਭੁਖਿਆ ਭੁਖ ਨ ਉਤਰੀ ਜੇ ਬੰਨਾ ਪੁਰੀਆ ਭਾਰ ॥
ਸਹਸ ਸਿਆਣਪਾ ਲਖ ਹੋਹਿ ਤ ਇਕ ਨ ਚਲੈ ਨਾਲਿ ॥
ਕਿਵ ਸਚਿਆਰਾ ਹੋਈਐ ਕਿਵ ਕੂੜੈ ਤੁਟੈ ਪਾਲਿ ॥
ਹੁਕਮਿ ਰਜਾਈ ਚਲਣਾ ਨਾਨਕ ਲਿਖਿਆ ਨਾਲਿ ॥੧॥

सोचै सोचि न होवई जे सोची लख वार ॥
चुपै चुप न होवई जे लाइ रहा लिव तार ॥
भुखिआ भुख न उतरी जे बन्ना पुरीआ भार ॥
सहस सिआणपा लख होहि त इक न चलै नालि ॥
किव सचिआरा होईऐ किव कूड़ै तुटै पालि ॥
हुकमि रजाई चलणा नानक लिखिआ नालि ॥१॥

1

Not by thought alone, Can He be known,

Though one think, A hundred thousand times; Not in solemn silence

Not in deep meditation. Though fasting yields an abundance of virtue

It cannot appease the hunger for truth. No, by none of these,

Nor by a hundred thousand other devices, Can God be reached.

How then shall the Truth be known? How the veil of false illusion torn?

O Nanak, thus runneth the writ divine, The righteous path – let it be thine.

ਹੁਕਮੀ ਹੋਵਨਿ ਆਕਾਰ ਹੁਕਮੁ ਨ ਕਹਿਆ ਜਾਈ ॥

ਹੁਕਮੀ ਹੋਵਨਿ ਜੀਅ ਹੁਕਮਿ ਮਿਲੈ ਵਡਿਆਈ ॥

ਹੁਕਮੀ ਉਤਮੁ ਨੀਚੁ ਹੁਕਮਿ ਲਿਖਿ ਦੁਖ ਸੁਖ ਪਾਈਅਹਿ ॥

ਇਕਨਾ ਹੁਕਮੀ ਬਖਸੀਸ ਇਕਿ ਹੁਕਮੀ ਸਦਾ ਭਵਾਈਅਹਿ ॥

ਹੁਕਮੈ ਅੰਦਰਿ ਸਭੁ ਕੋ ਬਾਹਰਿ ਹੁਕਮ ਨ ਕੋਇ ॥

ਨਾਨਕ ਹੁਕਮੈ ਜੇ ਬੁਝੈ ਤ ਹਉਮੈ ਕਹੈ ਨ ਕੋਇ ॥੨॥

हुकमी होवनि आकार हुकमु न कहिआ जाई ॥

हुकमी होवनि जीअ हुकमि मिलै वडिआई ॥

हुकमी उतमु नीचु हुकमि लिखि दुख सुख पाईअहि ॥

इकना हुकमी बखसीस इकि हुकमी सदा भवाईअहि ॥

हुकमै अंदरि सभु को बाहरि हुकम न कोइ ॥

नानक हुकमै जे बुझै त हउमै कहै न कोइ ॥२॥

2

By Him are all forms created,
By Him infused with life and blessed,

By him are some to excellence elated,
Others born lowly and depressed.

By His writ some have pleasure, others pain;
By His grace some are saved,

Others doomed to die, re-live, and die again.
His will encompasseth all, there be none beside.

O Nanak, He who knows, hath no ego and no pride.

ਗਾਵੈ ਕੋ ਤਾਣੁ ਹੋਵੈ ਕਿਸੈ ਤਾਣੁ ॥
ਗਾਵੈ ਕੋ ਦਾਤਿ ਜਾਣੈ ਨੀਸਾਣੁ ॥
ਗਾਵੈ ਕੋ ਗੁਣ ਵਡਿਆਈਆ ਚਾਰ ॥
ਗਾਵੈ ਕੋ ਵਿਦਿਆ ਵਿਖਮੁ ਵੀਚਾਰੁ ॥
ਗਾਵੈ ਕੋ ਸਾਜਿ ਕਰੇ ਤਨੁ ਖੇਹ ॥
ਗਾਵੈ ਕੋ ਜੀਅ ਲੈ ਫਿਰਿ ਦੇਹ ॥
ਗਾਵੈ ਕੋ ਜਾਪੈ ਦਿਸੈ ਦੂਰਿ ॥
ਗਾਵੈ ਕੋ ਵੇਖੈ ਹਾਦਰਾ ਹਦੂਰਿ ॥

गावै को ताणु होवै किसै ताणु ॥
गावै को दाति जाणै नीसाणु ॥
गावै को गुण वडिआई आ चार ॥
गावै को विदिआ विखमु वीचारु॥
गावै को साजि करे तनु खेह ॥
गावै को जीअ लै फिरि देह ॥
गावै को जापै दिसै दूरि ॥
गावै को वेखै हादरा हदूरि ॥

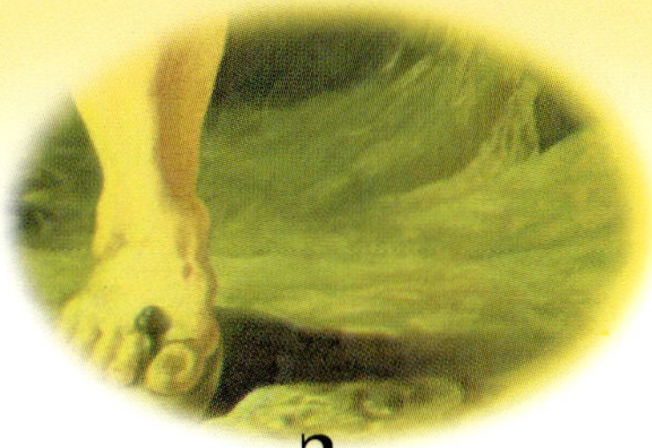

3

Who has the power to praise His might?Who has the measure of His bounty?

Of His portents who has the sight? Who can value His virtue, His deeds, His charity?

Who has the knowledge of his wisdom?Of His deep, impenetrable thought?

How worship Him who creates life, Then destroys,

And having destroyed doth re-create?

How worship Him who appeareth far

Yet is ever present and proximate?

ਕਥਨਾ ਕਥੀ ਨ ਆਵੈ ਤੋਟਿ ॥
ਕਥਿ ਕਥਿ ਕਥੀ ਕੋਟੀ ਕੋਟਿ ਕੋਟਿ ॥
ਦੇਦਾ ਦੇ ਲੈਦੇ ਥਕਿ ਪਾਹਿ ॥
ਜੁਗਾ ਜੁਗੰਤਰਿ ਖਾਹੀ ਖਾਹਿ ॥
ਹੁਕਮੀ ਹੁਕਮੁ ਚਲਾਏ ਰਾਹੁ ॥
ਨਾਨਕ ਵਿਗਸੈ ਵੇਪਰਵਾਹੁ ॥੩॥

कथना कथी न आवै तोटि ॥
कथि कथि कथी कोटी कोटि कोटि ॥
देदा दे लैदे थकि पाहि ॥
जुगा जुगंतरि खाही खाहि ॥
हुकमी हुकमु चलाए राहु ॥
नानक विगसै वेपरवाहु ॥३॥

There is no end to His description,
Though the speakers and their speeches be legion.
He the Giver ever giveth,
We who receive grow weary,
On His bounty humanity liveth
From primal age to posterity.

ਸਾਚਾ ਸਾਹਿਬੁ ਸਾਚੁ ਨਾਇ ਭਾਖਿਆ ਭਾਉ ਅਪਾਰੁ ॥
ਆਖਹਿ ਮੰਗਹਿ ਦੇਹਿ ਦੇਹਿ ਦਾਤਿ ਕਰੇ ਦਾਤਾਰੁ ॥
ਫੇਰਿ ਕਿ ਅਗੈ ਰਖੀਐ ਜਿਤੁ ਦਿਸੈ ਦਰਬਾਰੁ ॥
ਮੁਹੌਂ ਕਿ ਬੋਲਣੁ ਬੋਲੀਐ ਜਿਤੁ ਸੁਣਿ ਧਰੇ ਪਿਆਰੁ ॥
ਅੰਮ੍ਰਿਤ ਵੇਲਾ ਸਚੁ ਨਾਉ ਵਡਿਆਈ ਵਿਚਾਰੁ ॥
ਕਰਮੀ ਆਵੈ ਕਪੜਾ ਨਦਰੀ ਮੋਖੁ ਦੁਆਰੁ ॥
ਨਾਨਕ ਏਵੈ ਜਾਣੀਐ ਸਭੁ ਆਪੇ ਸਚਿਆਰੁ ॥੪॥

साचा साहिबु साचु नाइ भाखिआ भाउ अपारु॥
आखहि मंगहि देहि देहि दाति करे दातारु॥
फेरि कि अगै रखीऐ जितु दिसै दरबारु॥
मुहौ कि बोलणु बोलीऐ जितु सुणि धरे पिआरु॥
अंमृत वेला सचु नाउ वडिआई विचारु॥
करमी आवै कपड़ा नदरी मोखु दुआरु॥
नानक एवै जाणीऐ सभु आपे सचिआरु॥४॥

4

God is the master, God is truth, His name spelleth love divine,
His creatures ever cry: "O give, O give," He the bounteous doth never decline.
What then in offering shall we bring, That we may see his court above?
What then shall we say in speech, That hearing may evoke His love?
In the ambrosial hours of fragrant dawn, On truth and greatness ponder in meditation,
Though action determine how thou be born, Through grace alone comes salvation.
O Nanak, this need we know alone, That God and Truth are two in one.

ਥਾਪਿਆ ਨ ਜਾਇ ਕੀਤਾ ਨ ਹੋਇ ॥
ਆਪੇ ਆਪਿ ਨਿਰੰਜਨੁ ਸੋਇ ॥
ਜਿਨਿ ਸੇਵਿਆ ਤਿਨਿ ਪਾਇਆ ਮਾਨੁ ॥
ਨਾਨਕ ਗਾਵੀਐ ਗੁਣੀ ਨਿਧਾਨੁ ॥
ਗਾਵੀਐ ਸੁਣੀਐ ਮਨਿ ਰਖੀਐ ਭਾਉ ॥
ਦੁਖੁ ਪਰਹਰਿ ਸੁਖੁ ਘਰਿ ਲੈ ਜਾਇ ॥
ਗੁਰਮੁਖਿ ਨਾਦੰ ਗੁਰਮੁਖਿ ਵੇਦੰ
ਗੁਰਮੁਖਿ ਰਹਿਆ ਸਮਾਈ ॥

थापिआ न जाइ कीता न होइ ॥
आपे आपि निरंजनु सोइ ॥
जिनि सेविआ तिनि पाइआ मानु ॥
नानक गावीऐ गुणी निधानु ॥
गावीऐ सुणीऐ मनि रखीऐ भाउ ॥
दुखु परहरि सुखु घरि लै जाइ ॥
घुरमुखि नादं गुरमुखि वेदं
गुरमुखि रहिआ समाई ॥

5

He cannot be proved, for He is uncreated; He is without matter, self-existent.

They that serve shall honoured be, O Nanak, the Lord is most excellent.

Praise the Lord, hear them that do Him praise, In your hearts His name be graven,

Sorrows from your soul erase, And make your hearts a joyous haven.

The Guru's word has the sage's wisdom, The Guru's word is full of learning,

For though it be the Guru's word, God Himself speaks therein.

ਗੁਰੁ ਈਸਰੁ ਗੁਰੁ ਗੋਰਖੁ ਬਰਮਾ
ਗੁਰੁ ਪਾਰਬਤੀ ਮਾਈ ॥

ਜੇ ਹਉ ਜਾਣਾ ਆਖਾ ਨਾਹੀ
ਕਹਣਾ ਕਥਨੁ ਨ ਜਾਈ ॥

ਗੁਰਾ ਇਕ ਦੇਹਿ ਬੁਝਾਈ ॥

ਸਭਨਾ ਜੀਆ ਕਾ ਇਕੁ ਦਾਤਾ
ਸੋ ਮੈ ਵਿਸਰਿ ਨ ਜਾਈ ॥੫॥

गुरु ईसरु गुरु गोरखु बरमा
गुरु पारबती माई ॥

जे हउ जाणा आखा नाही
कहणा कथनु न जाई ॥

गुरा इक देहि बुझाई ॥

सभना जीआ का इकु दाता
सो मै विसरि न जाई ॥५॥

Thus run the words of the Guru:

"God is the destroyer, preserver and creator, God is the Goddess too.

Words to describe are hard to find, I would venture if I knew."

This alone my teacher taught,

There is but one Lord of all creation,

Forget him not.

ਤੀਰਥਿ ਨਾਵਾ ਜੇ ਤਿਸੁ ਭਾਵਾ
ਵਿਣੁ ਭਾਣੇ ਕਿ ਨਾਇ ਕਰੀ ॥
ਜੇਤੀ ਸਿਰਠਿ ਉਪਾਈ ਵੇਖਾ
ਵਿਣੁ ਕਰਮਾ ਕਿ ਮਿਲੈ ਲਈ ॥
ਮਤਿ ਵਿਚਿ ਰਤਨ ਜਵਾਹਰ ਮਾਣਿਕ
ਜੇ ਇਕ ਗੁਰ ਕੀ ਸਿਖ ਸੁਣੀ ॥
ਗੁਰਾ ਇਕ ਦੇਹਿ ਬੁਝਾਈ ॥
ਸਭਨਾ ਜੀਆ ਕਾ ਇਕੁ ਦਾਤਾ
ਸੋ ਮੈ ਵਿਸਰਿ ਨ ਜਾਈ ॥੬॥

तीरथि नावा जे तिसु भावा
विणु भाणे कि नाइ करी ॥
जेती सिरठि उपाई वेखा
विणु करमा कि मिलै लई ॥
मति विचि रतन जवाहर माणिक
जे इक गुर की सिख सुणी ॥
गुरा इक देहि बुझाई ॥
सभना जीआ का इकु दाता
सो मै विसरि न जाई ॥६॥

6

If it please the Lord, In holy waters would I bathe,
If it please him not, Worthless is that pilgrimage.
This is the law of all creation, That nothing's gained save by action.
Thy mind, wherein buried lie, Precious stones, jewels, gems,
Shall opened be if thou but try, And hearken to the Guru's word.
This the Guru my teacher taught,
There is but one Lord of all creation,
Forget Him not.

ਜੇ ਜੁਗ ਚਾਰੇ ਆਰਜਾ ਹੋਰ ਦਸੂਣੀ ਹੋਇ ॥
ਨਵਾ ਖੰਡਾ ਵਿਚਿ ਜਾਣੀਐ ਨਾਲਿ ਚਲੈ ਸਭੁ ਕੋਇ ॥
ਚੰਗਾ ਨਾਉ ਰਖਾਇ ਕੈ ਜਸੁ ਕੀਰਤਿ ਜਗਿ ਲੇਇ ॥
ਜੇ ਤਿਸੁ ਨਦਰਿ ਨ ਆਵਈ ਤ ਵਾਤ ਨ ਪੁਛੈ ਕੇ ॥
ਕੀਟਾ ਅੰਦਰਿ ਕੀਟੁ ਕਰਿ ਦੋਸੀ ਦੋਸੁ ਧਰੇ ॥
ਨਾਨਕ ਨਿਰਗੁਣਿ ਗੁਣੁ ਕਰੇ ਗੁਣਵੰਤਿਆ ਗੁਣੁ ਦੇ ॥
ਤੇਹਾ ਕੋਇ ਨ ਸੁਝਈ
ਜਿ ਤਿਸੁ ਗੁਣੁ ਕੋਇ ਕਰੇ ॥੭॥

जे जुग चारे आरजा होर दसूणी होइ ॥
नवा खंडा विचि जाणीऐ नालि चलै सभु कोइ ॥
चंगा नाउ रखाइ कै जसु कीरति जगि लेइ ॥
जे तिसु नदरि न आवई त वात न पुछै के ॥
कीटा अंदरि कीटु करि दोसी दोसु धरे ॥
नानक निरगुणि गुणु करे गुणवंतिआ गुणु दे ॥
तेहा कोइ न सुझई
जि तिसु गुणु कोइ करे ॥७॥

7

Were life's span extended to the four ages, And ten times more,

Were one known over the nine continents

Ever in humanity's fore, Were one to achieve greatness

With a name noised over the earth, If one found not favour with the Lord

What would it all be worth?

Among the worms be as vermin, By sinners be accused of sin.

O Nanak, the Lord fills the vicious with virtue, The virtuous maketh more true.

Knowest thou of any other, Who in turn could the Lord thus favour?

ਸੁਣਿਐ ਸਿਧ ਪੀਰ ਸੁਰਿ ਨਾਥ ॥
ਸੁਣਿਐ ਧਰਤਿ ਧਵਲ ਆਕਾਸ ॥
ਸੁਣਿਐ ਦੀਪ ਲੋਅ ਪਾਤਾਲ ॥
ਸੁਣਿਐ ਪੋਹਿ ਨ ਸਕੈ ਕਾਲੁ ॥
ਨਾਨਕ ਭਗਤਾ ਸਦਾ ਵਿਗਾਸੁ ॥
ਸੁਣਿਐ ਦੂਖ ਪਾਪ ਕਾ ਨਾਸੁ ॥੮॥

सुणिऐ सिध पीर सुरि नाथ ॥
सुणिऐ धरति धवल आकास ॥
सुणिऐ दीप लोअ पाताल ॥
सुणिऐ पोहि न सकै कालु ॥
नानक भगता सदा विगासु ॥
सुणिऐ दूख पाप का नासु ॥८॥

8

By hearing the word, Men achieve wisdom, saintliness, courage and contentment.

By hearing the word, Men learn of the earth, the power that, supports it and the firmament.

By hearing the word, Men learn of the upper and nether regions, of islands and continents.

By hearing the word, Men conquer the fear of death and the elements.

O Nanak, the word hath such magic for the worshippers,

Those that hear, death do not fear,

Their sorrows end and sins disappear.

ਸੁਣਿਐ ਈਸਰੁ ਬਰਮਾ ਇੰਦੁ ॥
ਸੁਣਿਐ ਮੁਖਿ ਸਾਲਾਹਣ ਮੰਦੁ ॥
ਸੁਣਿਐ ਜੋਗ ਜੁਗਤਿ ਤਨਿ ਭੇਦ ॥
ਸੁਣਿਐ ਸਾਸਤ ਸਿਮ੍ਰਿਤਿ ਵੇਦ ॥
ਨਾਨਕ ਭਗਤਾ ਸਦਾ ਵਿਗਾਸੁ ॥
ਸੁਣਿਐ ਦੂਖ ਪਾਪ ਕਾ ਨਾਸੁ ॥੯॥

सुणिऐ ईसरुबरमा इंदु ॥
सुणिऐ मुखि सालाहण मंदु ॥
सुणिऐ जोग जुगति तनि भेद ॥
सुणिऐ सासत सिमृति वेद ॥
नानक भगता सदा विगासु ॥
सुणिऐ दूख पाप का नासु ॥९॥

9

By hearing the word, Mortals are to godliness raised.

By hearing the word, The foul-mouthed are filled with pious praise.

By hearing the word, Are revealed the secrets of the body and of nature.

By hearing the word, Is acquired the wisdom of all the scriptures.

O Nanak, the word hath such magic for the worshippers,

Those that hear, death do not fear,

Their sorrows end and sins disappear.

ਸੁਣਿਐ ਸਤੁ ਸੰਤੋਖੁ ਗਿਆਨੁ ॥

ਸੁਣਿਐ ਅਠਸਠਿ ਕਾ ਇਸਨਾਨੁ ॥

ਸੁਣਿਐ ਪੜਿ ਪੜਿ ਪਾਵਹਿ ਮਾਨੁ ॥

ਸੁਣਿਐ ਲਾਗੈ ਸਹਜਿ ਧਿਆਨੁ ॥

ਨਾਨਕ ਭਗਤਾ ਸਦਾ ਵਿਗਾਸੁ ॥

ਸੁਣਿਐ ਦੂਖ ਪਾਪ ਕਾ ਨਾਸੁ ॥੧੦॥

सुणिऐ सतु संतोखु गिआनु ॥

सुणिऐ अठसठि का इसनानु ॥

सुणिऐ पड़ि पड़ि पावहि मानु ॥

सुणिऐ लागै सहजि धिआनु ॥

नानक भगता सदा विगासु ॥

सुणिऐ दूख पाप का नासु ॥१०॥

10

By hearing the word, One learns of truth, contentment, and is wise.

By hearing the word, The need for pilgrimages does not arise.

By hearing the word, The student achieves scholastic distinction.

By hearing the word, The mind is easily led to meditation.

O Nanak, the word hath such magic for the worshippers,

Those that hear, death do not fear,

Their sorrows end and sins disappear.

ਸੁਣਿਐ ਸਰਾ ਗੁਣਾ ਕੇ ਗਾਹ ॥
ਸੁਣਿਐ ਸੇਖ ਪੀਰ ਪਾਤਿਸਾਹ ॥
ਸੁਣਿਐ ਅੰਧੇ ਪਾਵਹਿ ਰਾਹੁ ॥
ਸੁਣਿਐ ਹਾਥ ਹੋਵੈ ਅਸਗਾਹੁ ॥
ਨਾਨਕ ਭਗਤਾ ਸਦਾ ਵਿਗਾਸੁ ॥
ਸੁਣਿਐ ਦੂਖ ਪਾਪ ਕਾ ਨਾਸੁ ॥੧੧॥

सुणिऐ सरा गुणा के गाह ॥
सुणिऐ सेख पीर पातिसाह ॥
सुणिऐ अंधे पावहि राहु ॥
सुणिऐ हाथ होवै असगाहु ॥
नानक भगता सदा विगासु ॥
सुणिऐ दूख पाप का नासु ॥११॥

11

By hearing the word, One sounds the depths of virtue's sea.

By hearing the word, One acquires learning, holiness and royalty.

By hearing the word, The blind see and their paths are visible.

By hearing the word, The fathomless becomes fordable.

O Nanak, the word hath such magic for the worshippers,

Those that hear, death do not fear,

Their sorrows end and sins disappear.

ਮੰਨੇ ਕੀ ਗਤਿ ਕਹੀ ਨ ਜਾਇ ॥

ਜੇ ਕੋ ਕਹੈ ਪਿਛੈ ਪਛੁਤਾਇ ॥

ਕਾਗਦਿ ਕਲਮ ਨ ਲਿਖਣਹਾਰੁ ॥

ਮੰਨੇ ਕਾ ਬਹਿ ਕਰਨਿ ਵੀਚਾਰੁ ॥

ਐਸਾ ਨਾਮੁ ਨਿਰੰਜਨੁ ਹੋਇ ॥

ਜੇ ਕੋ ਮੰਨਿ ਜਾਣੈ ਮਨਿ ਕੋਇ ॥੧੨॥

मन्ने की गति कही न जाइ ॥

जे को कहै पिछै पछुताइ ॥

कागदि कलम न लिखणहारु॥

मन्ने का बहि करनि वीचारु॥

ऐसा नामु निरंजनु होइ ॥

जे को मंनि जाणै मनि कोइ ॥१२॥

12

The believer's bliss one cannot describe,
He who endeavours regrets in the end,
There is no paper, pen, nor any scribe
Who can the believer's state comprehend.
The name of the Lord is immaculate.
He who would know must have faith.

ਮੰਨੈ ਸੁਰਤਿ ਹੋਵੈ ਮਨਿ ਬੁਧਿ ॥

ਮੰਨੈ ਸਗਲ ਭਵਣ ਕੀ ਸੁਧਿ ॥

ਮੰਨੈ ਮੁਹਿ ਚੋਟਾ ਨਾ ਖਾਇ ॥

ਮੰਨੈ ਜਮ ਕੈ ਸਾਥਿ ਨ ਜਾਇ ॥

ਐਸਾ ਨਾਮੁ ਨਿਰੰਜਨੁ ਹੋਇ ॥

ਜੇ ਕੋ ਮੰਨਿ ਜਾਣੈ ਮਨਿ ਕੋਇ ॥੧੩॥

मन्नै सुरति होवै मनि बुधि ॥

मन्नै सगल भवण की सुधि ॥

मन्नै मुहि चोटा ना खाइ ॥

मन्नै जम कै साथि न जाइ ॥

ऐसा नामु निरंजनु होइ ॥

जे को मंनि जाणै मनि कोइ ॥१३॥

13

The believer hath wisdom and understanding;

The believer hath knowledge of all the spheres;

The believer shall not stumble in ignorance,

Nor of death have any fears.

The name of the Lord is immaculate,

He who would know must have faith.

ਮੰਨੈ ਮਾਰਗਿ ਠਾਕ ਨ ਪਾਇ ॥

ਮੰਨੈ ਪਤਿ ਸਿਉ ਪਰਗਟੁ ਜਾਇ ॥

ਮੰਨੈ ਮਗੁ ਨ ਚਲੈ ਪੰਥੁ ॥

ਮੰਨੈ ਧਰਮ ਸੇਤੀ ਸਨਬੰਧੁ ॥

ਐਸਾ ਨਾਮੁ ਨਿਰੰਜਨੁ ਹੋਇ ॥

ਜੇ ਕੋ ਮੰਨਿ ਜਾਣੈ ਮਨਿ ਕੋਇ ॥੧੪॥

मन्नै मारगि ठाक न पाइ ॥

मन्नै पति सिउ परगटु जाइ ॥

मन्नै मगु न चलै पंथु ॥

मन्नै धरम सेती सनबंधु ॥

ऐसा नामु निरंजनु होइ ॥

जे को मंनि जाणै मनि कोइ ॥१४॥

14

The believer's way is of obstructions free;
The believer is honoured in the presence sublime;
The believer's path is not lost in futility,
For faith hath taught him law divine.
The name of the Lord is immaculate,
He who would know must have faith.

ਮੰਨੈ ਪਾਵਹਿ ਮੋਖੁ ਦੁਆਰੁ ॥
ਮੰਨੈ ਪਰਵਾਰੈ ਸਾਧਾਰੁ ॥
ਮੰਨੈ ਤਰੈ ਤਾਰੇ ਗੁਰੁ ਸਿਖ ॥
ਮੰਨੈ ਨਾਨਕ ਭਵਹਿ ਨ ਭਿਖ ॥
ਐਸਾ ਨਾਮੁ ਨਿਰੰਜਨੁ ਹੋਇ ॥
ਜੇ ਕੋ ਮੰਨਿ ਜਾਣੈ ਮਨਿ ਕੋਇ ॥੧੫॥

मन्नै पावहि मोखु दुआरु॥
मन्नै परवारै साधारु॥
मन्नै तरै तारे गुरुसिख ॥
मन्नै नानक भवहि न भिख ॥
ऐसा नामु निरंजनु होइ ॥
जे को मंनि जाणै मनि कोइ ॥१५॥

15

The believer reaches the gate of salvation;

His kith and kin he also saves.

The believer beckons the congregation,

Their souls are saved from transmigration

The name of the Lord is immaculate,

He who would know must have faith.

ਪੰਚ ਪਰਵਾਣ ਪੰਚ ਪਰਧਾਨੁ ॥
ਪੰਚੇ ਪਾਵਹਿ ਦਰਗਹਿ ਮਾਨੁ ॥
ਪੰਚੇ ਸੋਹਹਿ ਦਰਿ ਰਾਜਾਨੁ ॥
ਪੰਚਾ ਕਾ ਗੁਰੁ ਏਕੁ ਧਿਆਨੁ ॥
ਜੇ ਕੋ ਕਹੈ ਕਰੈ ਵਿਚਾਰੁ ॥
ਕਰਤੇ ਕੈ ਕਰਣੈ ਨਾਹੀ ਸੁਮਾਰੁ ॥
ਧੌਲੁ ਧਰਮੁ ਦਇਆ ਕਾ ਪੂਤੁ ॥
ਸੰਤੋਖੁ ਥਾਪਿ ਰਖਿਆ ਜਿਨਿ ਸੂਤਿ ॥

पंच परवाण पंच परधानु ॥
पंचे पावहि दरगहि मानु ॥
पंचे सोहहि दरि राजानु ॥
पंचा का गुरुएकु धिआनु ॥
जे को कहै करै विचारु॥
करते कै करणै नाही सुमारु॥
धौलु धरमु दइआ का पूतु ॥
संतोखु थापि रखिआ जिनि सूति ॥

16

Thus are chosen the leaders of men, Thus honoured in God's estimation;

Though they grace the courts of kings, Their minds are fixed in holy meditation.

Their words are weighed with reason, They know that God's works are legion.

Law which like the fabled bull supports the earth, Is of compassion born;

Though it bind the world in harmony, Its strands are thin and worn.

He who the truth would learn, Must know of the bull and the load it bore,

ਜੇ ਕੋ ਬੂਝੈ ਹੋਵੈ ਸਚਿਆਰੁ ॥
ਧਵਲੈ ਉਪਰਿ ਕੇਤਾ ਭਾਰੁ ॥
ਧਰਤੀ ਹੋਰੁ ਪਰੈ ਹੋਰੁ ਹੋਰੁ ॥
ਤਿਸ ਤੇ ਭਾਰੁ ਤਲੈ ਕਵਣੁ ਜੋਰੁ ॥
ਜੀਅ ਜਾਤਿ ਰੰਗਾ ਕੇ ਨਾਵ ॥
ਸਭਨਾ ਲਿਖਿਆ ਵੁੜੀ ਕਲਾਮ ॥
ਏਹੁ ਲੇਖਾ ਲਿਖਿ ਜਾਣੈ ਕੋਇ ॥
ਲੇਖਾ ਲਿਖਿਆ ਕੇਤਾ ਹੋਇ ॥

जे को बूझै होवै सचिआरु॥
धवलै उपरि केता भारु॥
धरती होरुपरै होरुहोरु॥
तिस ते भारुतलै कवणु जोरु॥
जीअ जाति रंगा के नाव ॥
सभना लिखिआ वुड़ी कलाम ॥
एहु लेखा लिखि जाणै कोइ ॥
लेखा लिखिआ केता होइ ॥

For there are worlds besides our own,
And beyond them many more.
Who is it that bears these burdens?
What power bears him that beareth them?
Of creatures of diverse kinds and colours,
The ever-flowing pen hath made record.
Can anyone write what it hath writ?

ਕੇਤਾ ਤਾਣੁ ਸੁਆਲਿਹੁ ਰੂਪੁ ॥

ਕੇਤੀ ਦਾਤਿ ਜਾਣੈ ਕੌਣੁ ਕੂਤੁ ॥

ਕੀਤਾ ਪਸਾਉ ਏਕੋ ਕਵਾਉ ॥

ਤਿਸ ਤੇ ਹੋਏ ਲਖ ਦਰੀਆਉ ॥

ਕੁਦਰਤਿ ਕਵਣ ਕਹਾ ਵੀਚਾਰੁ ॥

ਵਾਰਿਆ ਨ ਜਾਵਾ ਏਕ ਵਾਰ ॥

ਜੋ ਤੁਧੁ ਭਾਵੈ ਸਾਈ ਭਲੀ ਕਾਰ ॥

ਤੂ ਸਦਾ ਸਲਾਮਤਿ ਨਿਰੰਕਾਰ ॥੧੬॥

केता ताणु सुआलिहु रूपु ॥

केती दाति जाणै कौणु कूतु ॥

कीता पसाउ एको कवाउ ॥

तिस ते होए लख दरीआउ ॥

कुदरति कवण कहा वीचारु॥

वारिआ न जावा एक वार ॥

जो तुधु भावै साई भली कार ॥

तू सदा सलामति निरंकार ॥१६॥

Or say how great a task was it?

How describe His beauty and His might? His bounty how estimate?

How speak of Him who with one word, Did the whole universe create,

And made a thousand rivers flow therein? What might have I to praise Thy might?

I have not power to give it praise. Whatever be Thy wish, I say Amen.

Mayst Thou endure, O formless One.

ਅਸੰਖ ਜਪ ਅਸੰਖ ਭਾਉ ॥
ਅਸੰਖ ਪੂਜਾ ਅਸੰਖ ਤਪ ਤਾਉ ॥
ਅਸੰਖ ਗਰੰਥ ਮੁਖਿ ਵੇਦ ਪਾਠ ॥
ਅਸੰਖ ਜੋਗ ਮਨਿ ਰਹਹਿ ਉਦਾਸ ॥
ਅਸੰਖ ਭਗਤ ਗੁਣ ਗਿਆਨ ਵੀਚਾਰ ॥
ਅਸੰਖ ਸਤੀ ਅਸੰਖ ਦਾਤਾਰ ॥

असंख जप असंख भाउ ॥
असंख पूजा असंख तप ताउ ॥
असंख गरंथ मुखि वेद् पाठ ॥
असंख जोग मनि रहहि उदास ॥
असंख भगत गुण गिआन वीचार ॥
असंख सती असंख दातार ॥

17

There is no count of those who pray,

Nor of those who Thee adore;

There is no count of those who worship,

Nor of those who by penance set store.

There is no count of those who read the holy book aloud,

Nor of those who think of the world's sorrows and lament,

There is no count of sages immersed in thought and reason,

Nor of those who love humanity and are benevolent.

ਅਸੰਖ ਸੂਰ ਮੁਹ ਭਖ ਸਾਰ ॥

ਅਸੰਖ ਮੋਨਿ ਲਿਵ ਲਾਇ ਤਾਰ ॥

ਕੁਦਰਤਿ ਕਵਣ ਕਹਾ ਵਿਚਾਰੁ ॥

ਵਾਰਿਆ ਨ ਜਾਵਾ ਏਕ ਵਾਰ ॥

ਜੋ ਤੁਧੁ ਭਾਵੈ ਸਾਈ ਭਲੀ ਕਾਰ ॥

ਤੂ ਸਦਾ ਸਲਾਮਤਿ ਨਿਰੰਕਾਰ ॥੧੭॥

असंख सूर मुह भख सार ॥

असंख मोनि लिव लाइ तार ॥

कुदरति कवण कहा विचारु॥

वारिआ न जावा एक वार ॥

जो तुधु भावै साई भली कार ॥

तू सदा सलामति निरंकार ॥१७॥

There is no count of warriors who match their strength with steel,

Nor of those who contemplate in peace and are silent.

What might have I to praise Thy might?

I have not power to give it praise.

Whatever be Thy wish, I say Amen.

Mayst Thou endure, O formless One.

ਅਸੰਖ ਮੂਰਖ ਅੰਧ ਘੋਰ ॥

ਅਸੰਖ ਚੋਰ ਹਰਾਮਖੋਰ ॥

ਅਸੰਖ ਅਮਰ ਕਰਿ ਜਾਹਿ ਜੋਰ ॥

ਅਸੰਖ ਗਲਵਢ ਹਤਿਆ ਕਮਾਹਿ ॥

ਅਸੰਖ ਪਾਪੀ ਪਾਪੁ ਕਰਿ ਜਾਹਿ ॥

ਅਸੰਖ ਕੂੜਿਆਰ ਕੂੜੇ ਫਿਰਾਹਿ ॥

असंख मूरख अंध घोर ॥

असंख चोर हरामखोर ॥

असंख अमर करि जाहि जोर ॥

असंख गलवढ हतिआ कमाहि ॥

असंख पापी पापु करि जाहि ॥

असंख कूड़िआर कूड़े फिराहि ॥

18

There is no count of fools who will not see,

Nor of thieves who live by fraud,

There is no count of despots practising tyranny,

Nor of those whose hands are solied with blood.

There is no count of those who sin and go free,

Nor of liars caught in the web of falsehood,

ਅਸੰਖ ਮਲੇਛ ਮਲੁ ਭਖਿ ਖਾਹਿ ॥
ਅਸੰਖ ਨਿੰਦਕ ਸਿਰਿ ਕਰਹਿ ਭਾਰੁ ॥
ਨਾਨਕੁ ਨੀਚੁ ਕਹੈ ਵਿਚਾਰੁ ॥
ਵਾਰਿਆ ਨ ਜਾਵਾ ਏਕ ਵਾਰ ॥
ਜੋ ਤੁਧੁ ਭਾਵੈ ਸਾਈ ਭਲੀ ਕਾਰ ॥
ਤੂ ਸਦਾ ਸਲਾਮਤਿ ਨਿਰੰਕਾਰ ॥੧੮॥

असंख मलेछ मलु भखि खाहि ॥
असंख निंदक सिरि करहि भारु॥
नानकु नीचु कहै विचारु॥
वारिआ न जावा एक वार ॥
जो तुधु भावै साई भली कार ॥
तू सदा सलामति निरंकार ॥ १८॥

There is no count of the polluted who live on filth,
Nor of the evil-tongued weighed down with calumny.
Of such degradation, O Nanak, also think.
What might have I to praise Thy might?
I have not power to give it praise.
Whatever be Thy wish, I say Amen.
Mayst Thou endure, O formless One.

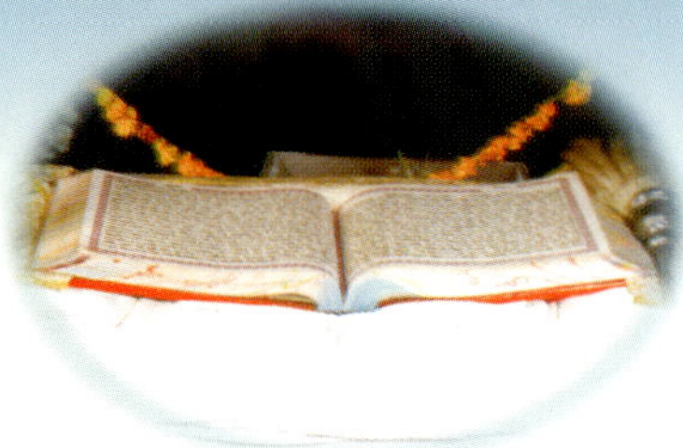

ਅਸੰਖ ਨਾਵ ਅਸੰਖ ਥਾਵ ॥

ਅਗੰਮ ਅਗੰਮ ਅਸੰਖ ਲੋਅ ॥

ਅਸੰਖ ਕਹਹਿ ਸਿਰਿ ਭਾਰੁ ਹੋਇ ॥

ਅਖਰੀ ਨਾਮੁ ਅਖਰੀ ਸਾਲਾਹ ॥

ਅਖਰੀ ਗਿਆਨੁ ਗੀਤ ਗੁਣ ਗਾਹ ॥

ਅਖਰੀ ਲਿਖਣੁ ਬੋਲਣੁ ਬਾਣਿ ॥

ਅਖਰਾ ਸਿਰਿ ਸੰਜੋਗੁ ਵਖਾਣਿ ॥

असंख नाव असंख थाव ॥

अगंम अगंम असंख लोअ ॥

असंख कहहि सिरि भारुहोइ ॥

अखरी नामु अखरी सालाह ॥

अखरी गिआनु गीत गुण गाह ॥

अखरी लिखणु बोलणु बाणि ॥

अखरा सिरि संजोगु वखाणि ॥

19

Though there is no count of Thy names and habitations,
Nor of Thy regions uncomprehended,
Yet many there have been with reason perverted,
Who to Thy knowledge have pretended.
Though by words alone we give Thee name and praise,
And by words reason, worship, and Thy virtue compute;
Though by words alone we write and speak,
And by words our ties with Thee constitute;

ਜਿਨਿ ਏਹਿ ਲਿਖੇ ਤਿਸੁ ਸਿਰਿ ਨਾਹਿ ॥

ਜਿਵ ਫੁਰਮਾਏ ਤਿਵ ਤਿਵ ਪਾਹਿ ॥

ਜੇਤਾ ਕੀਤਾ ਤੇਤਾ ਨਾਉ ॥

ਵਿਣੁ ਨਾਵੈ ਨਾਹੀ ਕੋ ਥਾਉ ॥

ਕੁਦਰਤਿ ਕਵਣ ਕਹਾ ਵੀਚਾਰੁ ॥

ਵਾਰਿਆ ਨ ਜਾਵਾ ਏਕ ਵਾਰ ॥

ਜੋ ਤੁਧੁ ਭਾਵੈ ਸਾਈ ਭਲੀ ਕਾਰ ॥

ਤੂ ਸਦਾ ਸਲਾਮਤਿ ਨਿਰੰਕਾਰ ॥੧੯॥

जिनि एहि लिखे तिसु सिरि नाहि ॥

जिव फुरमाए तिव तिव पाहि ॥

जेता कीता तेता नाउ ॥

विणु नावै नाही को थाउ ॥

कुदरति कवण कहा वीचारु॥

वारिआ न जावा एक वार ॥

जो तुधु भावै साई भली कार ॥

तू सदा सलामति निरंकार ॥१६॥

The word does not its Creator bind,

What Thou ordainest we receive.

Thy creations magnify Thee,

Thy name in all places find.

What might have I to praise Thy might?

I have not power to give it praise.

Whatever be thy wish, I say Amen.

Mayst Thou endure, O formless One.

ਭਰੀਐ ਹਥੁ ਪੈਰੁ ਤਨੁ ਦੇਹ ॥

ਪਾਣੀ ਧੋਤੈ ਉਤਰਸੁ ਖੇਹ ॥

ਮੂਤ ਪਲੀਤੀ ਕਪੜੁ ਹੋਇ ॥

ਦੇ ਸਾਬੂਣੁ ਲਈਐ ਓਹੁ ਧੋਇ ॥

ਭਰੀਐ ਮਤਿ ਪਾਪਾ ਕੈ ਸੰਗਿ ॥

ਓਹੁ ਧੋਪੈ ਨਾਵੈ ਕੈ ਰੰਗਿ ॥

भरीऐ हथु पैरुतनु देह ॥

पाणी धोतै उतरसु खेह ॥

मूत पलीती कपड़ु होइ ॥

दे साबूणु लईऐ ओहु धोइ ॥

भरीऐ मति पापा कै संगि ॥

ओहु धोपै नावै कै रंगि ॥

20

As hands or feet besmirched with slime,

Water washes white;

As garments dark with grime,

Rinsed with soap are made light;

So when sin soils the soul,

Prayer alone shall make it whole.

ਪੁੰਨੀ ਪਾਪੀ ਆਖਣੁ ਨਾਹਿ ॥
ਕਰਿ ਕਰਿ ਕਰਣਾ ਲਿਖਿ ਲੈ ਜਾਹੁ ॥
ਆਪੇ ਬੀਜਿ ਆਪੇ ਹੀ ਖਾਹੁ ॥
ਨਾਨਕ ਹੁਕਮੀ ਆਵਹੁ ਜਾਹੁ ॥੨੦॥

पुन्नी पापी आखणु नाहि ॥
करि करि करणा लिखि लै जाहु ॥
आपे बीजि आपे ही खाहु ॥
नानक हुकमी आवहु जाहु ॥२०॥

Words do not the saint or sinner make,
Action alone is written in the book of fate,
What we sow that alone we take;
O Nanak, be saved or for ever transmigrate.

ਤੀਰਥੁ ਤਪੁ ਦਇਆ ਦਤੁ ਦਾਨੁ ॥

ਜੇ ਕੋ ਪਾਵੈ ਤਿਲ ਕਾ ਮਾਨੁ ॥

ਸੁਣਿਆ ਮੰਨਿਆ ਮਨਿ ਕੀਤਾ ਭਾਉ ॥

ਅੰਤਰਗਤਿ ਤੀਰਥਿ ਮਲਿ ਨਾਉ ॥

ਸਭਿ ਗੁਣ ਤੇਰੇ ਮੈ ਨਾਹੀ ਕੋਇ ॥

ਵਿਣੁ ਗੁਣ ਕੀਤੇ ਭਗਤਿ ਨ ਹੋਇ ॥

तीरथु तपु दइआ दतु दानु ॥

जे को पावै तिल का मानु ॥

सुणिआ मंनिआ मनि कीता भाउ ॥

अंतरगति तीरथि मलि नाउ ॥

सभि गुण तेरे मै नाही कोइ ॥

विणु गुण कीते भगति न होइ ॥

21

Pilgrimage, austerity, mercy, almsgiving and charity,
Bring merit, be it as little as the mustard seed;
But he who hears, believes and cherishes the word,
An inner pilgrimage and cleansing is his meed.
All virtue is Thine, for I have none,
Virtue follows a good act done.

ਸੁਅਸਤਿ ਆਥਿ ਬਾਣੀ ਬਰਮਾਉ ॥

ਸਤਿ ਸੁਹਾਣੁ ਸਦਾ ਮਨਿ ਚਾਉ ॥

ਕਵਣੁ ਸੁ ਵੇਲਾ ਵਖਤੁ ਕਵਣੁ
ਕਵਣ ਥਿਤਿ ਕਵਣੁ ਵਾਰੁ ॥

ਕਵਣਿ ਸਿ ਰੁਤੀ ਮਾਹੁ ਕਵਣੁ ਜਿਤੁ ਹੋਆ ਆਕਾਰੁ ॥

ਵੇਲ ਨ ਪਾਈਆ ਪੰਡਤੀ ਜਿ ਹੋਵੈ ਲੇਖੁ ਪੁਰਾਣੁ ॥

ਵਖਤੁ ਨ ਪਾਇਓ ਕਾਦੀਆ
ਜਿ ਲਿਖਨਿ ਲੇਖੁ ਕੁਰਾਣੁ ॥

सुअसति आथि बाणी बरमाउ ॥

सति सुहाणु सदा मनि चाउ ॥

कवणु सु वेला वखतु कवणु
कवण थिति कवणु वारु॥

कवणि सि रुती माहु कवणु जितु होआ आकारु॥

वेल न पाईआ पंडती जि होवै लेखु पुराणु ॥

वखतु न पाइओ कादीआ
जि लिखनि लेखु कुराणु ॥

Blessed Thou the Creator, the prayer, the primal,
Truth and beauty and longing eternal.
What was the time, what day of the week,
What the month, what season of the year,
When Thou didst create the earthly sphere?
The Pandit knows it not, nor is it writ in his Puran;
The Qadi knows it not, though he read and copy the Koran.

ਥਿਤਿ ਵਾਰੁ ਨਾ ਜੋਗੀ ਜਾਣੈ ਰੁਤਿ ਮਾਹੁ ਨਾ ਕੋਈ ॥

ਜਾ ਕਰਤਾ ਸਿਰਠੀ ਕਉ ਸਾਜੇ ਆਪੇ ਜਾਣੈ ਸੋਈ ॥

ਕਿਵ ਕਰਿ ਆਖਾ ਕਿਵ ਸਾਲਾਹੀ
ਕਿਉ ਵਰਨੀ ਕਿਵ ਜਾਣਾ ॥

ਨਾਨਕ ਆਖਣਿ ਸਭੁ ਕੋ ਆਖੈ
ਇਕ ਦੂ ਇਕੁ ਸਿਆਣਾ ॥

ਵਡਾ ਸਾਹਿਬੁ ਵਡੀ ਨਾਈ ਕੀਤਾ ਜਾ ਕਾ ਹੋਵੈ ॥

ਨਾਨਕ ਜੇ ਕੋ ਆਪੌ ਜਾਣੈ
ਅਗੈ ਗਇਆ ਨ ਸੋਹੈ ॥੨੧॥

थिति वारुना जोगी जाणै रुति माहु ना कोई ॥

जा करता सिरठी कउ साजे आपे जाणै सोई ॥

किव करि आखा किव सालाही
किउ वरनी किव जाणा ॥

नानक आखणि सभु को आखै
इक दू इकु सिआणा ॥

वडा साहिबु वडी नाई कीता जा का होवै ॥

नानक जे को आपौ जाणै
अगै गइआ न सोहै ॥२१॥

The Yogi knows not the date nor the day of the week,

He knows not the month or even the season.

Only Thou who made it all can speak,

For knowledge is Thine alone.

How then shall I know Thee, how describe, praise and name?

O Nanak, many there be who pretend to know, each bolder in his claim.

All I say is: "Great is the Lord, great His name; What He ordains comes to be,"

O Nanak, he who sayeth more shall hereafter, regret his stupidity.

ਪਾਤਾਲਾ ਪਾਤਾਲ ਲਖ ਆਗਾਸਾ ਆਗਾਸ ॥
ਓੜਕ ਓੜਕ ਭਾਲਿ ਥਕੇ ਵੇਦ ਕਹਨਿ ਇਕ ਵਾਤ ॥
ਸਹਸ ਅਠਾਰਹ ਕਹਨਿ ਕਤੇਬਾ ਅਸੁਲੂ ਇਕੁ ਧਾਤੁ ॥
ਲੇਖਾ ਹੋਇ ਤ ਲਿਖੀਐ ਲੇਖੈ ਹੋਇ ਵਿਣਾਸੁ ॥
ਨਾਨਕ ਵਡਾ ਆਖੀਐ ਆਪੇ ਜਾਣੈ ਆਪੁ ॥੨੨॥

पाताला पाताल लख आगासा आगास ॥
ओड़क ओड़क भालि थके वेद कहनि इक वात ॥
सहस अठारह कहनि कतेबा असुलू इकु धातु ॥
लेखा होइ त लिखीऐ लेखै होइ विणासु ॥
नानक वडा आखीऐ आपे जाणै आपु ॥२२॥

22

Numerous worlds there be in regions beyond the skies and below,

But the research-weary scholars say, we do not know.

The Hindu and the Muslim books are full of theories; the answer is but one.

If it could be writ, it would have been, but the writer thereof be none.

O Nanak, say but this, the Lord is great, in His knowledge He is alone.

ਸਾਲਾਹੀ ਸਾਲਾਹਿ ਏਤੀ ਸੁਰਤਿ ਨ ਪਾਈਆ ॥

ਨਦੀਆ ਅਤੈ ਵਾਹ ਪਵਹਿ ਸਮੁੰਦਿ ਨ ਜਾਣੀਅਹਿ ॥

ਸਮੁੰਦ ਸਾਹ ਸੁਲਤਾਨ ਗਿਰਹਾ ਸੇਤੀ ਮਾਲੁ ਧਨੁ ॥

ਕੀੜੀ ਤੁਲਿ ਨ ਹੋਵਨੀ ਜੇ ਤਿਸੁ
ਮਨਹੁ ਨ ਵੀਸਰਹਿ ॥੨੩॥

सालाही सालाहि एती सुरति न पाईआ ॥

नदीआ अतै वाह पवहि समुंदि न जाणीअहि ॥

समुंद साह सुलतान गिरहा सेती मालु धनु ॥

कीड़ी तुलि न होवनी जे तिसु
मनहु न वीसरहि ॥२३॥

23

Worshippers who praise the Lord know not His greatness,
As rivers and rivulets that flow into the sea know not its vastness.
Mighty kings with domains vaster than the ocean,
With wealth piled high in a mountainous heap,
Are less than the little ant
That the Lord's name in its heart doth keep.

ਅੰਤੁ ਨ ਸਿਫਤੀ ਕਹਣਿ ਨ ਅੰਤੁ ॥

ਅੰਤੁ ਨ ਕਰਣੈ ਦੇਣਿ ਨ ਅੰਤੁ ॥

ਅੰਤੁ ਨ ਵੇਖਣਿ ਸੁਣਣਿ ਨ ਅੰਤੁ ॥

ਅੰਤੁ ਨ ਜਾਪੈ ਕਿਆ ਮਨਿ ਮੰਤੁ ॥

ਅੰਤੁ ਨ ਜਾਪੈ ਕੀਤਾ ਆਕਾਰੁ ॥

ਅੰਤੁ ਨ ਜਾਪੈ ਪਾਰਾਵਾਰੁ ॥

ਅੰਤ ਕਾਰਣਿ ਕੇਤੇ ਬਿਲਲਾਹਿ ॥

ਤਾ ਕੇ ਅੰਤ ਨ ਪਾਏ ਜਾਹਿ ॥

अंतु न सिफती कहणि न अंतु ॥

अंतु न करणै देणि न अंतु ॥

अंतु न वेखणि सुणणि न अंतु ॥

अंतु न जापै किआ मनि मंतु ॥

अंतु न जापै कीता आकारु॥

अंतु न जापै पारावारु॥

अंत कारणि केते बिललाहि ॥

ता के अंत न पाए जाहि ॥

24

Infinite His goodness, and the ways of exaltation;

Infinite His creation and His benefaction;

Infinite the sights and sounds, infinite His great design,

Infinite its execution, infinite without confine.

Many there be that cried in pain to seek the end of all ending.

Their cries were all in vain, for the end is past understanding.

ਏਹੁ ਅੰਤੁ ਨ ਜਾਣੈ ਕੋਇ ॥	एहु अंतु न जाणै कोइ ॥
ਬਹੁਤਾ ਕਹੀਐ ਬਹੁਤਾ ਹੋਇ ॥	बहुता कहीऐ बहुता होइ ॥
ਵਡਾ ਸਾਹਿਬੁ ਊਚਾ ਥਾਉ ॥	वडा साहिबु ऊचा थाउ ॥
ਊਚੇ ਉਪਰਿ ਊਚਾ ਨਾਉ ॥	ऊचे उपरि ऊचा नाउ ॥
ਏਵਡੁ ਊਚਾ ਹੋਵੈ ਕੋਇ ॥	एवडु ऊचा होवै कोइ ॥
ਤਿਸੁ ਊਚੇ ਕਉ ਜਾਣੈ ਸੋਇ ॥	तिसु ऊचे कउ जाणै सोइ ॥
ਜੇਵਡੁ ਆਪਿ ਜਾਣੈ ਆਪਿ ਆਪਿ ॥	जेवडु आपि जाणै आपि आपि ॥
ਨਾਨਕ ਨਦਰੀ ਕਰਮੀ ਦਾਤਿ ॥੨੪॥	नानक नदरी करमी दाति ॥२४॥

It is the end of which no one knoweth,
The more one says the more it groweth.
The Lord is of great eminence, exalted is His name.
He who would know His height, must in stature be the same.
He alone can His own greatness measure.
O Nanak, what He gives we must treasure.

ਬਹੁਤਾ ਕਰਮੁ ਲਿਖਿਆ ਨਾ ਜਾਇ ॥

ਵਡਾ ਦਾਤਾ ਤਿਲੁ ਨ ਤਮਾਇ ॥

ਕੇਤੇ ਮੰਗਹਿ ਜੋਧ ਅਪਾਰ ॥

ਕੇਤਿਆ ਗਣਤ ਨਹੀ ਵੀਚਾਰੁ ॥

ਕੇਤੇ ਖਪਿ ਤੁਟਹਿ ਵੇਕਾਰ ॥

ਕੇਤੇ ਲੈ ਲੈ ਮੁਕਰੁ ਪਾਹਿ ॥

ਕੇਤੇ ਮੂਰਖ ਖਾਹੀ ਖਾਹਿ ॥

ਕੇਤਿਆ ਦੂਖ ਭੂਖ ਸਦ ਮਾਰ ॥

बहुता करमु लिखिआ ना जाइ ॥

वडा दाता तिलु न तमाइ ॥

केते मंगहि जोध अपार ॥

केतिआ गणत नही वीचारु॥

केते खपि तुटहि वेकार ॥

केते लै लै मुकरुपाहि ॥

केते मूरख खाही खाहि ॥

केतिआ दूख भूख सद मार ॥

25

Of His bounty one cannot write too much,

He the great Giver desires not even a mustard seed;

Even the mighty beg at His door, and others such,

Whose numbers can never be conceived.

There be those who receive but are self-indulgent,

Others who get but have no gratitude.

There be the foolish whose bellies are never filled,

Others whom hunger's pain doth ever torment.

ਏਹਿ ਭਿ ਦਾਤਿ ਤੇਰੀ ਦਾਤਾਰ ॥

ਬੰਦਿ ਖਲਾਸੀ ਭਾਣੈ ਹੋਇ ॥

ਹੋਰੁ ਆਖਿ ਨ ਸਕੈ ਕੋਇ ॥

ਜੇ ਕੋ ਖਾਇਕੁ ਆਖਣਿ ਪਾਇ ॥

ਓਹੁ ਜਾਣੈ ਜੇਤੀਆ ਮੁਹਿ ਖਾਇ ॥

ਆਪੇ ਜਾਣੈ ਆਪੇ ਦੇਇ ॥

ਆਖਹਿ ਸਿ ਭਿ ਕੇਈ ਕੇਇ ॥

ਜਿਸ ਨੋ ਬਖਸੇ ਸਿਫਤਿ ਸਾਲਾਹ ॥

ਨਾਨਕ ਪਾਤਿਸਾਹੀ ਪਾਤਿਸਾਹੁ ॥੨੫॥

एहि भि दाति तेरी दातार ॥

बंदि खलासी भाणै होइ ॥

होरुआखि न सकै कोइ ॥

जे को खाइकु आखणि पाइ ॥

ओहु जाणै जेतीआ मुहि खाइ

आपे जाणै आपे देइ ॥

आखहि सि भि केई केइ ॥

जिस नो बखसे सिफति सालाह ॥

नानक पातिसाही पातिसाहु ॥२५॥

All this comes to pass as Thou hast willed.
Thy will alone breaks mortal bonds,
No one else hath influence.
The fool who argues otherwise,
Shall be smitten into silence.
The Lord knows our needs, and gives,
Few there be that count their blessings,
He who is granted gratitude and power to praise,
O Nanak, is the king of kings.

ਅਮੁਲ ਗੁਣ ਅਮੁਲ ਵਾਪਾਰ ॥

ਅਮੁਲ ਵਾਪਾਰੀਏ ਅਮੁਲ ਭੰਡਾਰ ॥

ਅਮੁਲ ਆਵਹਿ ਅਮੁਲ ਲੈ ਜਾਹਿ ॥

ਅਮੁਲ ਭਾਇ ਅਮੁਲਾ ਸਮਾਹਿ ॥

ਅਮੁਲੁ ਧਰਮੁ ਅਮੁਲੁ ਦੀਬਾਣੁ ॥

ਅਮੁਲੁ ਤੁਲੁ ਅਮੁਲੁ ਪਰਵਾਣੁ ॥

अमुल गुण अमुल वापार ॥

अमुल वापारीए अमुल भंडार ॥

अमुल आवहि अमुल लै जाहि ॥

अमुल भाइ अमुला समाहि ॥

अमुलु धरमु अमुलु दीबाणु ॥

अमुलु तुलु अमुलु परवाणु ॥

26

His goodness cannot be priced or traded,
Nor His worshippers valued, not their store;
Priceless too are dealers in the market sacred
With love and peace evermore.
Perfect His law and administration,
Precise His weights and measures;

ਅਮੁਲੁ ਬਖਸੀਸ ਅਮੁਲੁ ਨੀਸਾਣੁ ॥

ਅਮੁਲੁ ਕਰਮੁ ਅਮੁਲੁ ਫੁਰਮਾਣੁ ॥

ਅਮੁਲੋ ਅਮੁਲੁ ਆਖਿਆ ਨ ਜਾਇ ॥

ਆਖਿ ਆਖਿ ਰਹੇ ਲਿਵ ਲਾਇ ॥

ਆਖਹਿ ਵੇਦ ਪਾਠ ਪੁਰਾਣ ॥

ਆਖਹਿ ਪੜੇ ਕਰਹਿ ਵਖਿਆਣ ॥

अमुलु बखसीस अमुलु नीसाणु ॥

अमुलु करमु अमुलु फुरमाणु ॥

अमुलो अमुलु आखिआ न जाइ ॥

आखि आखि रहे लिव लाइ ॥

आखहि वेद् पाठ पुराण ॥

आखहि पड़े करहि वखिआण ॥

Boundless His bounty and His omens,
Infinite mercy in His orders.
How priceless Thou art one cannot state,
Those who spoke are mute in adoration,
The readers of the scriptures expatiate,
Having read, are lost in learned conversation.

ਆਖਹਿ ਬਰਮੇ ਆਖਹਿ ਇੰਦ ॥	आखहि बरमे आखहि इंद ॥
ਆਖਹਿ ਗੋਪੀ ਤੈ ਗੋਵਿੰਦ ॥	आखहि गोपी तै गोविंद ॥
ਆਖਹਿ ਈਸਰ ਆਖਹਿ ਸਿਧ ॥	आखहि ईसर आखहि सिध ॥
ਆਖਹਿ ਕੇਤੇ ਕੀਤੇ ਬੁਧ ॥	आखहि केते कीते बुध ॥
ਆਖਹਿ ਦਾਨਵ ਆਖਹਿ ਦੇਵ ॥	आखहि दानव आखहि देव ॥
ਆਖਹਿ ਸੁਰਿ ਨਰ ਮੁਨਿ ਜਨ ਸੇਵ ॥	आखहि सुरि नर मुनि जन सेव ॥

The great gods Brahma and Indra do Thee proclaim,
So do Krishna and his maidens fair;
Siva and the Saivites do Thee name;
The Buddhas Thou made, Thy name bear.
The demons and the demi-gods
Men, brave men, seers and the sainted,

ਕੇਤੇ ਆਖਹਿ ਆਖਣਿ ਪਾਹਿ ॥

ਕੇਤੇ ਕਹਿ ਕਹਿ ਉਠਿ ਉਠਿ ਜਾਹਿ ॥

ਏਤੇ ਕੀਤੇ ਹੋਰਿ ਕਰੇਹਿ ॥

ਤਾ ਆਖਿ ਨ ਸਕਹਿ ਕੇਈ ਕੇਇ ॥

ਜੇਵਡੁ ਭਾਵੈ ਤੇਵਡੁ ਹੋਇ ॥

ਨਾਨਕ ਜਾਣੈ ਸਾਚਾ ਸੋਇ ॥

ਜੇ ਕੋ ਆਖੈ ਬੋਲੁਵਿਗਾੜੁ ॥

ਤਾ ਲਿਖੀਐ ਸਿਰਿ ਗਾਵਾਰਾ ਗਾਵਾਰੁ ॥੨੬॥

केते आखहि आखणि पाहि ॥

केते कहि कहि उठि उठि जाहि ॥

एते कीते होरि करेहि ॥

ता आखि न सकहि केई केइ ॥

जेवडु भावै तेवडु होइ ॥

नानक जाणै साचा सोइ ॥

जे को आखै बोलुविगाड़ु ॥

ता लिखीऐ सिरि गावारा गावारु॥२६॥

Having discoursed and discussed
Have spoken and departed.
If Thou didst many more create
Not one could any more state,
For Thou art as great as is Thy pleasure,
O Nanak, Thou alone knowest Thy measure.
He who claims to know blasphemeth
And is the worst among the stupidest.

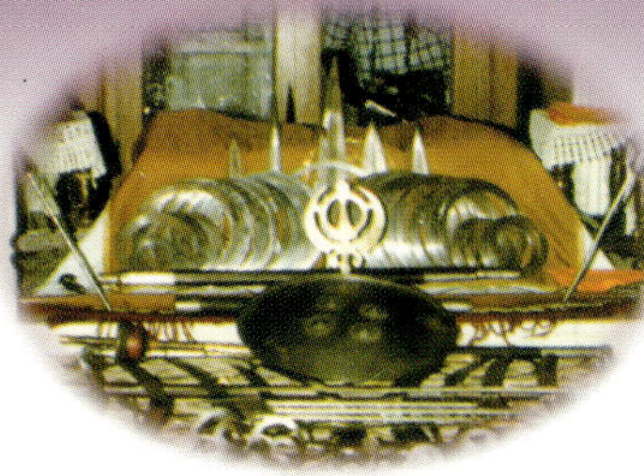

ਸੋ ਦਰੁ ਕੇਹਾ ਸੋ ਘਰੁ ਕੇਹਾ ਜਿਤੁ ਬਹਿ
ਸਰਬ ਸਮਾਲੇ ॥

ਵਾਜੇ ਨਾਦ ਅਨੇਕ ਅਸੰਖਾ ਕੇਤੇ ਵਾਵਣਹਾਰੇ ॥

ਕੇਤੇ ਰਾਗ ਪਰੀ ਸਿਉ ਕਹੀਅਨਿ ਕੇਤੇ ਗਾਵਣਹਾਰੇ ॥

ਗਾਵਹਿ ਤੁਹਨੋ ਪਉਣੁ ਪਾਣੀ ਬੈਸੰਤਰੁ
ਗਾਵੈ ਰਾਜਾ ਧਰਮੁ ਦੁਆਰੇ ॥

ਗਾਵਹਿ ਚਿਤੁ ਗੁਪਤੁ ਲਿਖਿ ਜਾਣਹਿ ਲਿਖਿ ਲਿਖਿ
ਧਰਮੁ ਵੀਚਾਰੇ ॥

सो दरुकेहा सो घरुकेहा जितु बहि
सरब समाले ॥

वाजे नाद अनेक असंखा केते वावणहारे ॥

केते राग परी सिउ कहीअनि केते गावणहारे ॥

गावहि तुहनो पउणु पाणी बैसंतरु
गावै राजा धरमु दुआरे ॥

गावहि चितु गुपतु लिखि जाणहि लिखि लिखि
धरमु वीचारे ॥

27

SODAR

(Te Deum)

Where is the gate, where the mansion, From whence Thou watchest all creation,

Where sounds of musical melodies, Of instruments playing, minstrels singing,

Are joined in divine harmony? There the breezes blow, the waters run and the fires burn,

There Dharmaraj, the king of death, sits in state; There the recording angles Chitra and Gupta write

For Dharmaraj to read and adjudicate.

ਗਾਵਹਿ ਈਸਰੁ ਬਰਮਾ ਦੇਵੀ ਸੋਹਨਿ ਸਦਾ ਸਵਾਰੇ ॥

ਗਾਵਹਿ ਇੰਦ ਇਦਾਸਣਿ ਬੈਠੇ ਦੇਵਤਿਆ
ਦਰਿ ਨਾਲੇ ॥

ਗਾਵਹਿ ਸਿਧ ਸਮਾਧੀ ਅੰਦਰਿ ਗਾਵਨਿ
ਸਾਧ ਵਿਚਾਰੇ ॥

ਗਾਵਨਿ ਜਤੀ ਸਤੀ ਸੰਤੋਖੀ ਗਾਵਹਿ ਵੀਰ ਕਰਾਰੇ ॥

ਗਾਵਨਿ ਪੰਡਿਤ ਪੜਨਿ ਰਖੀਸਰ
ਜੁਗੁ ਜੁਗੁ ਵੇਦਾ ਨਾਲੇ ॥

गावहि ईसरुबरमा देवी सोहनि सदा सवारे ॥

गावहि इंद इदासणि बैठे देवतिआ
दरि नाले ॥

गावहि सिध समाधी अंदरि गावनि
साध विचारे ॥

गावनि जती सती संतोखी गावहि वीर करारे ॥

गावनि पंडित पड़नि रखीसर
जुगु जुगु वेदा नाले ॥

There are the gods Ishwara and Brahma, The goddess Devi of divine grace;

There Indra sits on his celestial throne, And lesser gods, each in his place.

There ascetics in deep meditation, Holy men in contemplation,

The pure of heart, the continent,

Men of peace and contentment, Doughty warriors never yielding,

Thy praises are ever singing. From age to age, the pundit and the sage

Do Thee exalt in their study and their writing.

ਗਾਵਹਿ ਮੋਹਣੀਆ ਮਨੁ ਮੋਹਨਿ ਸੁਰਗਾ
ਮਛ ਪਇਆਲੇ ॥
ਗਾਵਨਿ ਰਤਨ ਉਪਾਏ ਤੇਰੇ ਅਠਸਠਿ ਤੀਰਥ ਨਾਲੇ ॥
ਗਾਵਹਿ ਜੋਧ ਮਹਾਬਲ ਸੂਰਾ ਗਾਵਹਿ ਖਾਣੀ ਚਾਰੇ ॥
ਗਾਵਹਿ ਖੰਡ ਮੰਡਲ ਵਰਭੰਡਾ ਕਰਿ ਕਰਿ ਰਖੇ ਧਾਰੇ ॥

गावहि मोहणीआ मनु मोहनि सुरगा
मछ पइआले ॥
गावनि रतन उपाए तेरे अठसठि तीरथ नाले ॥
गावहि जोध महाबल सूरा गावहि खाणी चारे ॥
गावहि खंड मंडल वरभंडा करि करि रखे धारे ॥

There maidens fair, heart bewitching,

Who inhabit the earth, the upper and the lower regions, Thy praises chant in their singing.

By the gems that Thou didst create, In the sixty-eight places of pilgrimage,

Is Thy name exalted. By warriors strong and brave in strife,

By the sources four from whence came life,

Of egg or womb, of sweat or seed, Is Thy name magnified.

The regions of the earth, the heavens and the universe

ਸੋਈ ਤੁਧੁਨੋ ਗਾਵਹਿ ਜੋ ਤੁਧੁ ਭਾਵਨਿ ਰਤੇ ਤੇਰੇ
ਭਗਤ ਰਸਾਲੇ ॥

ਹੋਰ ਕੇਤੇ ਗਾਵਨਿ ਸੇ ਮੈ ਚਿਤਿ ਨ ਆਵਨਿ ਨਾਨਕੁ
ਕਿਆ ਵੀਚਾਰੇ ॥

ਸੋਈ ਸੋਈ ਸਦਾ ਸਚੁ ਸਾਹਿਬੁ ਸਾਚਾ ਸਾਚੀ ਨਾਈ ॥

सेई तुधुनो गावहि जो तुधु भावनि रते तेरे
भगत रसाले ॥

होर केते गावनि से मै चिति न आवनि नानकु
किआ वीचारे ॥

सोई सोई सदा सचु साहिबु साचा साची नाई ॥

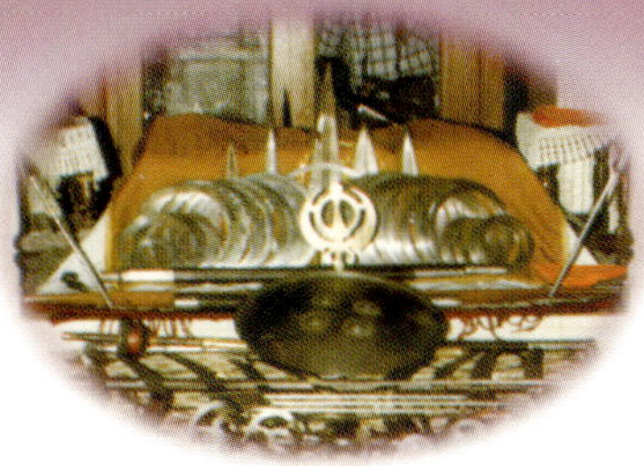

That Thou didst make and dost sustain, Sing to Thee and praise Thy name.

Only those Thou lovest and with whom Thou art pleased

Can give Thee praise and in Thy love be steeped.

Others too there must be who Thee acclaim, I have no memory of knowing them

Nor of knowledge, O Nanak, make a claim.

He alone is the master true, Lord of the word, ever the same,

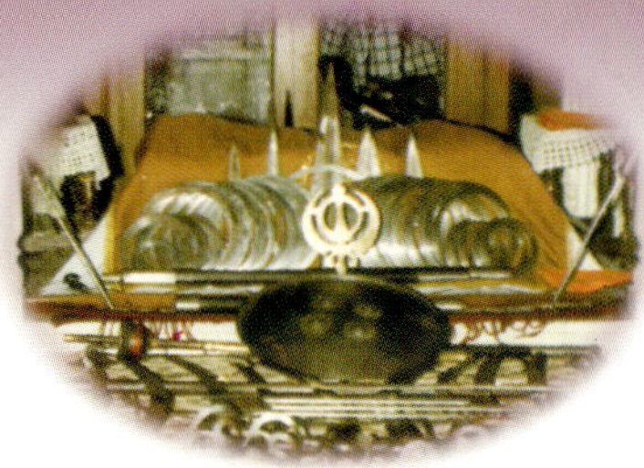

ਹੈ ਭੀ ਹੋਸੀ ਜਾਇ ਨ ਜਾਸੀ ਰਚਨਾ ਜਿਨਿ ਰਚਾਈ ॥

ਰੰਗੀ ਰੰਗੀ ਭਾਤੀ ਕਰਿ ਕਰਿ ਜਿਨਸੀ
ਮਾਇਆ ਜਿਨਿ ਉਪਾਈ ॥

ਕਰਿ ਕਰਿ ਵੇਖੈ ਕੀਤਾ ਆਪਣਾ
ਜਿਵ ਤਿਸ ਦੀ ਵਡਿਆਈ ॥

ਜੋ ਤਿਸੁ ਭਾਵੈ ਸੋਈ ਕਰਸੀ
ਹੁਕਮੁ ਨ ਕਰਣਾ ਜਾਈ॥

ਸੋ ਪਾਤਿਸਾਹੁ ਸਾਹਾ ਪਾਤਿਸਾਹਿਬੁ
ਨਾਨਕ ਰਹਣੁ ਰਜਾਈ ॥੨੭॥

है भी होसी जाइ न जासी रचना जिनि रचाई ॥

रंगी रंगी भाती करि करि जिनसी
माइआ जिनि उपाई ॥

करि करि वेखै कीता आपणा
जिव तिस दी वडिआई ॥

जो तिसु भावै सोई करसी
हुकमु न करणा जाई ॥

सो पातिसाहु साहा पातिसाहिबु
नानक रहणु रजाई ॥२७॥

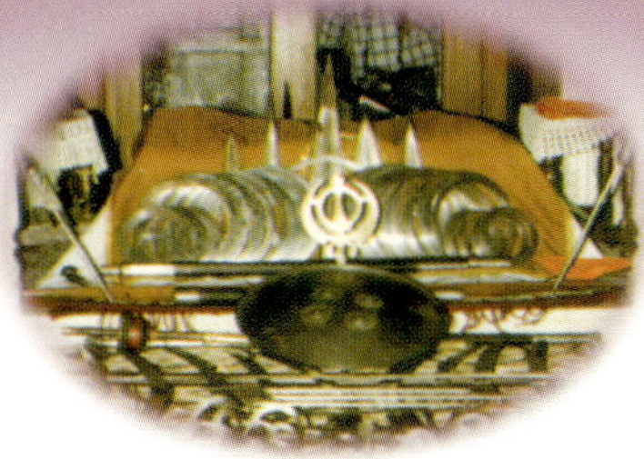

He Who made creation is, shall be and shall ever remain;

He Who made things of diverse species, shapes and hues,

Beholds that His handiwork His greatness proves.

What He wills He ordains,

To Him no one can an order give,

For He, O Nanak, is the King of Kings,

As He wills so we must live.

ਮੁੰਦਾ ਸੰਤੋਖੁ ਸਰਮੁ ਪਤੁ ਝੋਲੀ
ਧਿਆਨ ਕੀ ਕਰਹਿ ਬਿਭੂਤਿ ॥
ਖਿੰਥਾ ਕਾਲੁ ਕੁਆਰੀ ਕਾਇਆ
ਜੁਗਤਿ ਡੰਡਾ ਪਰਤੀਤਿ ॥
ਆਈ ਪੰਥੀ ਸਗਲ ਜਮਾਤੀ

मुंदा संतोखु सरमु पतु झोली
धिआन की करहि बिभूति ॥
खिंथा कालु कुआरी काइआ
जुगति डंडा परतीति ॥
आई पंथी सगल जमाती

28

As a beggar goes a-begging,
Bowl in one hand, staff in the other,
Rings in his ears, in ashes smothered,
So go thou forth in life.
With earrings made of contentment,
With modesty thy begging bowl,
Meditation the fabric of thy garment,
Knowledge of death thy cowl.
Let thy mind be chaste, virginal clean,

ਮਨਿ ਜੀਤੈ ਜਗੁ ਜੀਤੁ ॥

ਆਦੇਸੁ ਤਿਸੈ ਆਦੇਸੁ ॥

ਆਦਿ ਅਨੀਲੁ ਅਨਾਦਿ ਅਨਾਹਤਿ
ਜੁਗੁ ਜੁਗੁ ਏਕੋ ਵੇਸੁ ॥੨੮॥

मनि जीतै जगु जीतु ॥

आदेसु तिसै आदेसु ॥

आदि अनीलु अनादि अनाहति
जुगु जुगु एको वेसु ॥२८॥

Faith the staff on which to lean.[1]

Thou shalt then thy fancy humiliate

With mind subdued, the word subjugate.

Hail! and to thee be salutation.

Thou art primal, Thou art pure,

Without beginning, without termination,

In single form, for ever endure.

[1] In the original, the author makes reference to the "Ayee Panth,"

ਭੁਗਤਿ ਗਿਆਨੁ ਦਇਆ ਭੰਡਾਰਣਿ
ਘਟਿ ਘਟਿ ਵਾਜਹਿ ਨਾਦ ॥
ਆਪਿ ਨਾਥੁ ਨਾਥੀ ਸਭ ਜਾ ਕੀ ਰਿਧਿ ਸਿਧਿ
ਅਵਰਾ ਸਾਦ ॥
ਸੰਜੋਗੁ ਵਿਜੋਗੁ ਦੁਇ ਕਾਰ
ਚਲਾਵਹਿ ਲੇਖੇ ਆਵਹਿ ਭਾਗ ॥
ਆਦੇਸੁ ਤਿਸੈ ਆਦੇਸੁ ॥
ਆਦਿ ਅਨੀਲੁ ਅਨਾਦਿ ਅਨਾਹਤਿ
ਜੁਗੁ ਜੁਗੁ ਏਕੋ ਵੇਸੁ ॥੨੯॥

भुगति गिआनु दइआ भंडारणि
घटि घटि वाजहि नाद ॥
आपि नाथु नाथी सभ जा की रिधि सिधि
अवरा साद ॥
संजोगु विजोगु दुइ कार
चलावहि लेखे आवहि भाग ॥
आदेसु तिसै आदेसु ॥
आदि अनीलु अनादि अनाहति
जुगु जुगुएको वेसु ॥२९॥

29

From the store-house of compassion

Seek knowledge for thy food.

Let thy heart-beat be the call of the conchshell, Blown in gratitude.

He is the Lord, His is the will, His the creation,

He is the master of destiny, of union and separation.

Hail! and to thee be salutation.

Thou art primal, thou art pure,

Without beginning, without termination,

In single form, for ever endure.

ਏਕਾ ਮਾਈ ਜੁਗਤਿ ਵਿਆਈ ਤਿਨਿ ਚੇਲੇ ਪਰਵਾਣੁ ॥

ਇਕੁ ਸੰਸਾਰੀ ਇਕੁ ਭੰਡਾਰੀ ਇਕੁ ਲਾਏ ਦੀਬਾਣੁ ॥

ਜਿਵ ਤਿਸੁ ਭਾਵੈ ਤਿਵੈ ਚਲਾਵੈ
ਜਿਵ ਹੋਵੈ ਫੁਰਮਾਣੁ ॥

ਓਹੁ ਵੇਖੈ ਓਨਾ ਨਦਰਿ ਨ ਆਵੈ
ਬਹੁਤਾ ਏਹੁ ਵਿਡਾਣੁ ॥

ਆਦੇਸੁ ਤਿਸੈ ਆਦੇਸੁ ॥

ਆਦਿ ਅਨੀਲੁ ਅਨਾਦਿ ਅਨਾਹਤਿ
ਜੁਗੁ ਜੁਗੁ ਏਕੋ ਵੇਸੁ ॥੩੦॥

एका माई जुगति विआई तिनि चेले परवाणु ॥

इकु संसारी इकु भंडारी इकु लाए दीबाणु ॥

जिव तिसु भावै तिवै चलावै
जिव होवै फुरमाणु ॥

ओहु वेखै ओना नदरि न आवै
बहुता एहु विडाणु ॥

आदेसु तिसै आदेसु ॥

आदि अनीलु अनादि अनाहति
जुगु जुगु एको वेसु ॥३०॥

30

Maya, mythical goddess in wedlock divine, Bore three gods accepted by all,

The creator of the world, the one who preserves, And the one who adjudges its fall.

But it is God alone whose will prevails, Others but their obedience render.

He sees and directs, but is by them unseen, That of all is the greatest wonder.

Hail! and to Thee be salutation.

Thou art primal, thou art pure, Without beginning, without termination,

In single form, for ever endure.

ਆਸਣੁ ਲੋਇ ਲੋਇ ਭੰਡਾਰ ॥

ਜੋ ਕਿਛੁ ਪਾਇਆ ਸੁ ਏਕਾ ਵਾਰ ॥

ਕਰਿ ਕਰਿ ਵੇਖੈ ਸਿਰਜਣਹਾਰੁ ॥

ਨਾਨਕ ਸਚੇ ਕੀ ਸਾਚੀ ਕਾਰ ॥

ਆਦੇਸੁ ਤਿਸੈ ਆਦੇਸੁ ॥

ਆਦਿ ਅਨੀਲੁ ਅਨਾਦਿ ਅਨਾਹਤਿ
ਜੁਗੁ ਜੁਗੁ ਏਕੋ ਵੇਸੁ ॥੩੧॥

आसणु लोइ लोइ भंडार ॥

जो किछु पाइआ सु एका वार ॥

करि करि वेखै सिरजणहारु॥

नानक सचे की साची कार ॥

आदेसु तिसै आदेसु ॥

आदि अनीलु अनादि अनाहति
जुगु जुगु एको वेसु ॥३१॥

31

He hath His prayer-mat in every region, In every realm His store.

To human beings He doth apportion, Their share for once and evermore.

The Maker having made doth His own creation view.

O Nanak, He made truth itself, for He himself is true.

Hail! and to thee be salutation.

Thou are primal, thou art pure,

Without beginning, without termination,

In single form, for ever endure.

ਇਕ ਦੂ ਜੀਭੌ ਲਖ ਹੋਹਿ ਲਖ ਹੋਵਹਿ ਲਖ ਵੀਸ ॥

ਲਖੁ ਲਖੁ ਗੇੜਾ ਆਖੀਅਹਿ ਏਕੁ ਨਾਮੁ ਜਗਦੀਸ ॥

ਏਤੁ ਰਾਹਿ ਪਤਿ ਪਵੜੀਆ ਚੜੀਐ ਹੋਇ ਇਕੀਸ ॥

ਸੁਣਿ ਗਲਾ ਆਕਾਸ ਕੀ ਕੀਟਾ ਆਈ ਰੀਸ ॥

ਨਾਨਕ ਨਦਰੀ ਪਾਈਐ ਕੂੜੀ ਕੂੜੈ ਠੀਸ ॥੩੨॥

इक दू जीभौ लख होहि लख होवहि लख वीस ॥

लखु लखु गेड़ा आखीअहि एकु नामु जगदीस ॥

एतु राहि पति पवड़ीआ चड़ीऐ होइ इकीस ॥

सुणि गला आकास की कीटा आई रीस ॥

नानक नदरी पाईऐ कूड़ी कूड़ै ठीस ॥३२॥

32

Were I given a hundred thousand tongues instead of one,

And the hundred thousand multiplied twenty-fold,

A hundred thousand times would I say, and say again,

The Lord of all the worlds is one.

That is the path that leads, These the steps that mount,

Ascend thus to the Lord's mansion, And with Him be joined in unison.

The sound of the songs of heaven thrills, The like of us who crawl, but desire to fly.

O Nanak, His grace alone it is that fulfills, The rest mere prattle, and a lie.

ਆਖਣਿ ਜੋਰੁ ਚੁਪੈ ਨਹ ਜੋਰੁ ॥
ਜੋਰੁ ਨ ਮੰਗਣਿ ਦੇਣਿ ਨ ਜੋਰੁ ॥
ਜੋਰੁ ਨ ਜੀਵਣਿ ਮਰਣਿ ਨਹ ਜੋਰੁ ॥
ਜੋਰੁ ਨ ਰਾਜਿ ਮਾਲਿ ਮਨਿ ਸੋਰੁ ॥
ਜੋਰੁ ਨ ਸੁਰਤੀ ਗਿਆਨਿ ਵੀਚਾਰਿ ॥
ਜੋਰੁ ਨ ਜੁਗਤੀ ਛੁਟੈ ਸੰਸਾਰੁ ॥
ਜਿਸੁ ਹਥਿ ਜੋਰੁ ਕਰਿ ਵੇਖੈ ਸੋਇ ॥
ਨਾਨਕ ਉਤਮੁ ਨੀਚੁ ਨ ਕੋਇ ॥੩੩॥

आखणि जोरुचुपै नह जोरु॥
जोरुन मंगणि देणि न जोरु॥
जोरुन जीवणि मरणि नह जोरु॥
जोरुन राजि मालि मनि सोरु॥
जोरुन सुरती गिआनि वीचारि ॥
जोरुन जुगती छुटै संसारु॥
जिसु हथि जोरुकरि वेखै सोइ ॥
नानक उतमु नीचु न कोइ ॥३३॥

33

Ye have no power to speak or in silence listen,

To grant or give away,

Ye have no power to live or die.

Ye have no power to acquire wealth and dominion,

To compel the mind to thought or reason,

To escape the world and fly.

He who hath the pride of power, let him try and see.

O Nanak, before the Lord there is no low or high degree.

ਰਾਤੀ ਰੁਤੀ ਥਿਤੀ ਵਾਰ ॥

ਪਵਣ ਪਾਣੀ ਅਗਨੀ ਪਾਤਾਲ ॥

ਤਿਸੁ ਵਿਚਿ ਧਰਤੀ ਥਾਪਿ ਰਖੀ ਧਰਮ ਸਾਲ ॥

ਤਿਸੁ ਵਿਚਿ ਜੀਅ ਜੁਗਤਿ ਕੇ ਰੰਗ ॥

ਤਿਨ ਕੇ ਨਾਮ ਅਨੇਕ ਅਨੰਤ ॥

ਕਰਮੀ ਕਰਮੀ ਹੋਇ ਵੀਚਾਰੁ ॥

ਸਚਾ ਆਪਿ ਸਚਾ ਦਰਬਾਰੁ ॥

राती रुती थिती वार ॥

पवण पाणी अगनी पाताल ॥

तिसु विचि धरती थापि रखी धरम साल ॥

तिसु विचि जीअ जुगति के रंग ॥

तिन के नाम अनेक अन्नत ॥

करमी करमी होइ वीचारु॥

सचा आपि सचा दरबारु॥

34

He Who made the night and day, The days of the week and the seasons,

He who made the breezes blow, the waters run, The fires and the lower regions,

Made the earth – the temple of law.

He Who made creatures of diverse kinds, With a multitude of names,

Made this the law – By thought and deed be judged forsooth,

For God is true and dispenseth truth.

ਤਿਥੈ ਸੋਹਨਿ ਪੰਚ ਪਰਵਾਣੁ ॥

ਨਦਰੀ ਕਰਮਿ ਪਵੈ ਨੀਸਾਣੁ ॥

ਕਚ ਪਕਾਈ ਓਥੈ ਪਾਇ ॥

ਨਾਨਕ ਗਇਆ ਜਾਪੈ ਜਾਇ ॥੩੪॥

तिथै सोहनि पंच परवाणु ॥

नदरी करमि पवै नीसाणु ॥

कच पकाई ओथै पाइ ॥

नानक गइआ जापै जाइ ॥३४॥

There the elect His court adorn,
And God Himself their actions honours;
There are sorted deeds that were done and bore fruit
From those that to action could never ripen.
This, O Nanak, shall hereafter happen.

ਧਰਮ ਖੰਡ ਕਾ ਏਹੋ ਧਰਮੁ ॥

ਗਿਆਨ ਖੰਡ ਕਾ ਆਖਹੁ ਕਰਮੁ ॥

ਕੇਤੇ ਪਵਣ ਪਾਣੀ ਵੈਸੰਤਰ ਕੇਤੇ ਕਾਨ ਮਹੇਸ ॥

ਕੇਤੇ ਬਰਮੇ ਘਾੜਤਿ ਘੜੀਅਹਿ ਰੂਪ ਰੰਗ ਕੇ ਵੇਸ ॥

ਕੇਤੀਆ ਕਰਮ ਭੂਮੀ ਮੇਰ ਕੇਤੇ ਕੇਤੇ ਧੂ ਉਪਦੇਸ ॥

ਕੇਤੇ ਇੰਦ ਚੰਦ ਸੂਰ ਕੇਤੇ ਕੇਤੇ ਮੰਡਲ ਦੇਸ ॥

धरम खंड का एहो धरमु ॥

गिआन खंड का आखहु करमु ॥

केते पवण पाणी वैसंतर केते कान महेस ॥

केते बरमे घाड़ति घड़ीअहि रूप रंग के वेस ॥

केतीआ करम भूमी मेर केते केते धू उपदेस ॥

केते इंद चंद सूर केते केते मंडल देस ॥

35

In the realm of justice there is law;
In the realm of knowledge there is reason.
Wherefore are the breezes, the water and fire,
Gods that preserve and destroy, Krishnas and Shivas?
Wherefore are created forms, colours, attire,
Gods that create, the many Brahmas?
Here one strives to comprehend,
The golden mount of knowledge ascend,
And learn as did the sage Dhruva.

ਕੇਤੇ ਸਿਧ ਬੁਧ ਨਾਥ ਕੇਤੇ ਕੇਤੇ ਦੇਵੀ ਵੇਸ ॥
ਕੇਤੇ ਦੇਵ ਦਾਨਵ ਮੁਨਿ ਕੇਤੇ ਕੇਤੇ ਰਤਨ ਸਮੁੰਦ ॥
ਕੇਤੀਆ ਖਾਣੀ ਕੇਤੀਆ ਬਾਣੀ ਕੇਤੇ ਪਾਤ ਨਰਿੰਦ ॥
ਕੇਤੀਆ ਸੁਰਤੀ ਸੇਵਕ
ਕੇਤੇ ਨਾਨਕ ਅੰਤੁ ਨ ਅੰਤੁ ॥੩੫॥

केते सिध बुध नाथ केते केते देवी वेस ॥
केते देव दानव मुनि केते केते रतन समुंद ॥
केतीआ खाणी केतीआ बाणी केते पात नरिंद ॥
केतीआ सुरती सेवक
केते नानक अंतु न अंतु ॥३५॥

Wherefore are the thunders and lightning,
The moons and suns, The world and its regions?
Wherefore are the sages, seers, wise men,
Goddesses, false prophets, demons and demigods,
Wherefore are there jewels in the ocean?
How many forms of life there be, How many tongues, How many kings of proud ancestry.
Of these things many strive to know,
Many the slaves of reason. Many there are, O Nanak, their numbers are legion.

ਗਿਆਨ ਖੰਡ ਮਹਿ ਗਿਆਨੁ ਪਰਚੰਡੁ ॥

ਤਿਥੈ ਨਾਦ ਬਿਨੋਦ ਕੋਡ ਅਨੰਦੁ ॥

ਸਰਮ ਖੰਡ ਕੀ ਬਾਣੀ ਰੂਪੁ ॥

ਤਿਥੈ ਘਾੜਤਿ ਘੜੀਐ ਬਹੁਤੁ ਅਨੂਪੁ ॥

ਤਾ ਕੀਆ ਗਲਾ ਕਥੀਆ ਨਾ ਜਾਹਿ ॥

ਜੇ ਕੋ ਕਹੈ ਪਿਛੈ ਪਛੁਤਾਇ ॥

ਤਿਥੈ ਘੜੀਐ ਸੁਰਤਿ ਮਤਿ ਮਨਿ ਬੁਧਿ ॥

ਤਿਥੈ ਘੜੀਐ ਸੁਰਾ ਸਿਧਾ ਕੀ ਸੁਧਿ ॥੩੬॥

गिआन खंड महि गिआनु परचंडु ॥

तिथै नाद् बिनोद् कोड अन्नदु ॥

सरम खंड की बाणी रूपु ॥

तिथै घाड़ति घड़ीऐ बहुतु अनूपु ॥

ता कीआ गला कथीआ ना जाहि ॥

जे को कहै पिछै पछुताइ ॥

तिथै घड़ीऐ सुरति मति मनि बुधि ॥

तिथै घड़ीऐ सुरा सिधा की सुधि ॥३६॥

36

As in the realm of knowledge reason is triumphant
And yields a myriad joys,
So in the realm of bliss is beauty resplendent.
There are fashioned forms of great loveliness;
Of them it is best to remain silent
Than hazard guesses and then repent.
There too are fashioned consciousness, understanding, mind and reason,
The genius of the sage and seer, the power of humans superhuman.

ਕਰਮ ਖੰਡ ਕੀ ਬਾਣੀ ਜੋਰੁ ॥

ਤਿਥੈ ਹੋਰੁ ਨ ਕੋਈ ਹੋਰੁ ॥

ਤਿਥੈ ਜੋਧ ਮਹਾਬਲ ਸੂਰ ॥

ਤਿਨ ਮਹਿ ਰਾਮੁ ਰਹਿਆ ਭਰਪੂਰ ॥

ਤਿਥੈ ਸੀਤੋ ਸੀਤਾ ਮਹਿਮਾ ਮਾਹਿ ॥

ਤਾ ਕੇ ਰੂਪ ਨ ਕਥਨੇ ਜਾਹਿ ॥

करम खंड की बाणी जोरु॥

तिथै होरुन कोई होरु॥

तिथै जोध महाबल सूर ॥

तिन महि रामु रहिआ भरपूर ॥

तिथै सीतो सीता महिमा माहि ॥

ता के रूप न कथने जाहि ॥

37

In the realm of action, effort is supreme,
Nothing else prevails.
There dwell doughty warriors brave and strong,
With hearts full of godliness,
And celestial maidens of great loveliness
Who sing their praise.

ਨਾ ਓਹਿ ਮਰਹਿ ਨ ਠਾਗੇ ਜਾਹਿ ॥

ਜਿਨ ਕੈ ਰਾਮੁ ਵਸੈ ਮਨ ਮਾਹਿ ॥

ਤਿਥੈ ਭਗਤ ਵਸਹਿ ਕੇ ਲੋਅ ॥

ਕਰਹਿ ਅਨੰਦੁ ਸਚਾ ਮਨਿ ਸੋਇ ॥

ਸਚ ਖੰਡਿ ਵਸੈ ਨਿਰੰਕਾਰੁ ॥

ਕਰਿ ਕਰਿ ਵੇਖੈ ਨਦਰਿ ਨਿਹਾਲ ॥

ना ओहि मरहि न ठागे जाहि ॥

जिन कै रामु वसै मन माहि ॥

तिथै भगत वसहि के लोअ ॥

करहि अन्नदु सचा मनि सोइ ॥

सच खंडि वसै निरंकारु॥

करि करि वेखै नदरि निहाल ॥

They cannot die nor be beguiled,
For God Himself in their hearts resides.
There too are congregations of holy men
Who rejoice, for the Lord in their midst presides.
In the realm of truth is the Formless One
Who, having created, watches His creation
And graces us with the blessed vision.

ਤਿਥੈ ਖੰਡ ਮੰਡਲ ਵਰਭੰਡ ॥

ਜੇ ਕੋ ਕਥੈ ਤ ਅੰਤ ਨ ਅੰਤ ॥

ਤਿਥੈ ਲੋਅ ਲੋਅ ਆਕਾਰ ॥

ਜਿਵ ਜਿਵ ਹੁਕਮੁ ਤਿਵੈ ਤਿਵ ਕਾਰ ॥

ਵੇਖੈ ਵਿਗਸੈ ਕਰਿ ਵੀਚਾਰੁ ॥

ਨਾਨਕ ਕਥਨਾ ਕਰੜਾ ਸਾਰੁ ॥੩੭॥

तिथै खंड मंडल वरभंड ॥

जे को कथै त अंत न अंत ॥

तिथै लोअ लोअ आकार ॥

जिव जिव हुकमु तिवै तिव कार ॥

वेखै विगसै करि वीचारु॥

नानक कथना करड़ा सारु॥३७॥

There are the lands, the earths and the spheres
Of whose description there is no limit;
There by a myriad forms are a myriad purposes fulfilled,
What He ordains is in them instilled.
What He beholds, thinks and contemplates,
O Nanak, is too hard to state.

ਜਤੁ ਪਾਹਾਰਾ ਧੀਰਜੁ ਸੁਨਿਆਰੁ ॥
ਅਹਰਣਿ ਮਤਿ ਵੇਦੁ ਹਥੀਆਰੁ ॥
ਭਉ ਖਲਾ ਅਗਨਿ ਤਪ ਤਾਉ ॥
ਭਾਂਡਾ ਭਾਉ ਅੰਮ੍ਰਿਤੁ ਤਿਤੁ ਢਾਲਿ ॥
ਘੜੀਐ ਸਬਦੁ ਸਚੀ ਟਕਸਾਲ ॥
ਜਿਨ ਕਉ ਨਦਰਿ ਕਰਮੁ ਤਿਨ ਕਾਰ ॥
ਨਾਨਕ ਨਦਰੀ ਨਦਰਿ ਨਿਹਾਲ ॥੩੮॥

जतु पाहारा धीरजु सुनिआरु॥
अहरणि मति वेदु हथीआरु॥
भउ खला अगनि तप ताउ ॥
भाँडा भाउ अंमृतु तितु ढालि ॥
घड़ीऐ सबदु सची टकसाल ॥
जिन कउ नदरि करमु तिन कार ॥
नानक नदरी नदरि निहाल ॥३८॥

38

If thou must make a gold coin true, Let thy mint these rules pursue.

In the forge of continence, Let the goldsmith be a man of patience,

His tools be made of knowledge, His anvil made of reason;

With the fear of God the bellows blow, With prayer and austerity make the fire glow.

Pour the liquid in the mould of love, Print the name of the Lord thereon,

And cool it in the holy waters.

For thus in the mint of truth the word is coined, Thus those who are graced are to work enjoined.

O Nanak, by His blessing have joy ever lasting.

ਸਲੋਕੁ ॥

ਪਵਣੁ ਗੁਰੂ ਪਾਣੀ ਪਿਤਾ ਮਾਤਾ ਧਰਤਿ ਮਹਤੁ ॥
ਦਿਵਸੁ ਰਾਤਿ ਦੁਇ ਦਾਈ ਦਾਇਆ
ਖੇਲੈ ਸਗਲ ਜਗਤੁ ॥
ਚੰਗਿਆਈਆ ਬੁਰਿਆਈਆ ਵਾਚੈ ਧਰਮੁ ਹਦੂਰਿ ॥
ਕਰਮੀ ਆਪੋ ਆਪਣੀ ਕੇ ਨੇੜੈ ਕੇ ਦੂਰਿ ॥
ਜਿਨੀ ਨਾਮੁ ਧਿਆਇਆ ਗਏ ਮਸਕਤਿ ਘਾਲਿ ॥
ਨਾਨਕ ਤੇ ਮੁਖ ਉਜਲੇ ਕੇਤੀ ਛੁਟੀ ਨਾਲਿ ॥੧॥

सलोकु ॥

पवणु गुरूपाणी पिता माता धरति महतु ॥
दिवसु राति दुइ दाई दाइआ
खेलै सगल जगतु ॥
चंगिआईआ बुरिआईआ वाचै धरमु हदूरि ॥
करमी आपो आपणी के नेड़ै के दूरि ॥
जिनी नामु धिआइआ गए मसकति घालि ॥
नानक ते मुख उजले केती छुटी नालि ॥१॥

SHLOK (Epilogue)

Air, water and earth, Of these are we made. Air like the Guru's word gives the breath of life
To the babe born to the great mother earth, Sired by the waters. The day and night our nurses be
That watch us in our infancy. In their laps we play. The world is our playground.
Our acts right and wrong at Thy court shall come to judgment,
Some be seated near Thy seat, some ever kept distant.
The toils have ended of those that have worshipped Thee,
O Nanak, their faces are lit with joyful radiance, many others they set free.